Toni Castillo Girona

**Mum comes home twice a week**

Toni Castillo Girona

# Mum comes home twice a week

## and other stories

JustFiction Edition

**Impressum/Imprint (nur für Deutschland/only for Germany)**
Bibliografische Information der Deutschen Nationalbibliothek: Die Deutsche Nationalbibliothek verzeichnet diese Publikation in der Deutschen Nationalbibliografie; detaillierte bibliografische Daten sind im Internet über http://dnb.d-nb.de abrufbar.
Alle in diesem Buch genannten Marken und Produktnamen unterliegen warenzeichen-, marken- oder patentrechtlichem Schutz bzw. sind Warenzeichen oder eingetragene Warenzeichen der jeweiligen Inhaber. Die Wiedergabe von Marken, Produktnamen, Gebrauchsnamen, Handelsnamen, Warenbezeichnungen u.s.w. in diesem Werk berechtigt auch ohne besondere Kennzeichnung nicht zu der Annahme, dass solche Namen im Sinne der Warenzeichen- und Markenschutzgesetzgebung als frei zu betrachten wären und daher von jedermann benutzt werden dürften.

Coverbild: www.ingimage.com

Verlag: JustFiction! Edition ist ein Imprint der
LAP LAMBERT Academic Publishing GmbH & Co. KG
Heinrich-Böcking-Str. 6-8, 66121 Saarbrücken, Deutschland
Telefon +49 681 37 20 310, Telefax +49 681 37 20 310-9
Email: info@justfiction-edition.com

Herstellung in Deutschland:
Schaltungsdienst Lange o.H.G., Berlin
Books on Demand GmbH, Norderstedt
Reha GmbH, Saarbrücken
Amazon Distribution GmbH, Leipzig
**ISBN: 978-3-8454-4504-5**

**Imprint (only for USA, GB)**
Bibliographic information published by the Deutsche Nationalbibliothek: The Deutsche Nationalbibliothek lists this publication in the Deutsche Nationalbibliografie; detailed bibliographic data are available in the Internet at http://dnb.d-nb.de.
Any brand names and product names mentioned in this book are subject to trademark, brand or patent protection and are trademarks or registered trademarks of their respective holders. The use of brand names, product names, common names, trade names, product descriptions etc. even without a particular marking in this works is in no way to be construed to mean that such names may be regarded as unrestricted in respect of trademark and brand protection legislation and could thus be used by anyone.

Cover image: www.ingimage.com

Publisher: JustFiction! Edition
is an imprint of the publishing house
LAP LAMBERT Academic Publishing GmbH & Co. KG
Heinrich-Böcking-Str. 6-8, 66121 Saarbrücken, Germany
Phone +49 681 37 20 310, Fax +49 681 37 20 310-9
Email: info@justfiction-edition.com

Printed in the U.S.A.
Printed in the U.K. by (see last page)
**ISBN: 978-3-8454-4504-5**

# Table of Contents

# THE GIFTS

1

I thought I knew him; but I have to admit I was terribly mistaken. That man, that kind person I considered as my friend, after all those years, turned out to be a stranger. My recalls and memories of that time are blurry, but I can say for certain he was the best friend ever. And now, what's left? Merely a remembrance; images vanishing in the thin air as soon as I try to keep them strongly.

Before he died, he made me swear I would take care of her. We were out for a walk; it was a bright warm day, indeed. There was no one to be seen; at first I thought we were the only ones wandering around immersed in such memoirs. At that precise moment he said to me: *The day I die, you have to look after her.* I was truly mystified about those words he had spoken. I didn't know her, not to mention the fact she didn't know me. Not being aware of each other, how in the world was I supposed to take care of her? I asked him, but he shrugged and continued walking, as if he was absolutely certain I would find the way.

That day I felt odd. I went home pretty tired; there was no one waiting for me, so I decided to watch a movie and then go have a good rest. I tried not to think about what he just said to me, but it turned out quite difficult to accomplish. I suppose I knew something weird was going to happen, but I could barely figure it out. When I was falling asleep, the phone rang. It was him. *What's wrong?* I asked him; during what looked like the best part of a minute, there was only silence. Then, all of a sudden I could hear his voice, merely being a whisper: *Don't forget about the gifts.*

The day after I went to pay him a visit. I was worried, and I came to realize he could be down in the mouth, thus I woke up early in the morning and, just before going to work, I set foot in his building. I rang the bell, but it seemed he was out. Mystified, I tried to call him using my cell; no answer. It was pointless to be standing there, awaiting him, so I decided to go to work and try him later.

While being at work, I received a phone call. It was him. *Where have you been?* I think I asked him. He didn't even try to excuse himself; again I heard his sick voice, *They are all priceless, you know that.* I was shocked. What was he talking about? By *they* I could fathom he was referring to those gifts, but it was so weird. After another pause, he said to me: *You've got the key.* Right after saying that, he hang up. I called him back, but I got no answer. That evening, I left my job really concerned , so I walked all the way down to his flat. It was then I saw the police and one huge ambulance standing in front of the building. I knew almost immediately he was dead. The lights of that ambulance illuminated the surroundings, which in turn were getting dark because of the nightfall. The dusk, I think I thought, the dusk. The perfect moment to find out my friend had killed himself.

I was dead right. While watching what was happening around me, some girl approached me and, staring at my sad face, she realized I was some sort of a friend of his. She took one of my hands and whispered: *He shot himself.* It was all over. I didn't know that girl, but I came to know she belonged to the ambulance personnel because of how she dressed. She tried to make me get calm, and I don't know for sure, but I think I cried silently. I noticed a sweet and warm finger drying my tears, which were running down my cheeks. I didn't look at her, or at least I can't recall doing that, but surely I was more or less grateful and I do know I tried to say something to her, to utter some sort of pleasantries, but nothing came out in the end. Then, she dissapeared and I stayed there completely alone and lonely, despite the fact there was a crowd in a hell of a situation, doing this and doing that, while another kind of enormous crowd was standing beside and behind me, looking at all that mess truly interested, as if they were watching a film, one of those ones which seem real, thinking probably it was all too far from their own lives.

I came back home feeling shit. *Shit happens.* It was true. I started going upstairs so as to reach my flat but first I checked my mailbox out. In there there was an envelope with my name impressed on it. I grabbed it and opened it. Inside, just a short hand-written letter and a key. I could recognize that key; it was *his* key, the key to open *his* door. I read the letter quickly, right there, standing in front of my opened mailbox.

> *Now, you have the key as I promised.*
> *Don't forget about the gifts.*
> *Find her, and take her to them.*
> *It's important, do me that favour.*
> *My time has come, but hers is yet to come.*
>
> > *So long,*
> > *your friend.*

I read that letter two or three times, trying to determine the real meaning of that nonsense. I could not. I put it inside my pocket and went upstairs. It was a calm night, and I could even hear the silence. I shut my door and went to bed almost immediately, letting my heavy body fall down tiredly. At that time I thought I was going to be extremely depressed, devastated. I knew it for sure. Slowly, amidst the darkest hours of my entire life, surrounded by memoirs and feeling for the first time what sadness really meant, I let my body drown in the dream, in one of those ones anyone wishes to be, because they are all sweet and make you feel you are, once and for all, *yourself.*

2

I met her some rainy day of October. Oh, she was pretty: she still is. I could find out where she lived at the time because of some notes my friend left me in his laptop. At first I was not sure how I could conduct such a meeting. Bear in mind I didn't know what she knew about my friend, those gifts, these odd events implying suicide. I thought it could be better to spend some time gathering information about her, in order to be prepared to face such a moment. There were abundant clues about how she could be and what she could look like. My friend had pictures of her in his laptop, and an impressive huge collection of email messages. I read them all, and I came to realize she was not only pretty, she was an angel. Then I understood why he loved her intensively, and I felt sad. I tried to make up my mind, find some useful information and go find her. When I phoned her, she was shocked. I tried to explain myself clearly, and she got it in the right way. We decided to meet each other one October morning,  in a *café* not too far from her neighbourhood.

I spent an hour wandering around that very morning. I was in no hurry,  trying to think hard about what could end up happening. When I arrived at the café, I could see her inside. She was seated, with a cup of coffee between her hands, gazing at some point I could hardly identify. Apart from her, there were no more customers. I decided not to enter immediately, thus I stayed out there surveying her passionately. She was black-haired and every now and again she was lifting her cup up so as to sip some coffee. Despite the fact it was a downpour, I had no problems at all being there, outside the *café*, getting piss wet as long as I could be analysing her, watching her movements, feeling terribly sad because of my friend's death, hoping she could even know me deeply, now that my friend was dead. I knew it was awful. But I couldn't help it. She was pretty, indeed. And all I knew at that very moment was I would like to meet her *right away* but, obviously, to keep meeting her for years, no matter what.

Finally, I set foot on the café. I reached her. *Hello, it's me.* She looked up: *Nice to meet you.* I sat down and started to talk to her. She stared at me inquisitively, listening to me carefully, trying not to miss a word. I told her all I knew about my friend, his letter, those gifts of his. I told her I got the key to his flat, so I could give it to her if she wanted to, or I could accompany her to his flat and figure all of this out together. In fact, I hoped she would decide to come along, but I could not tell her that. *It's okay, I'm coming with you,* she said to me finally. Glad as I was, I smiled and went to pay for the coffees, then we both got out of the café and in no time we were headed to my dead friend's flat.

After his death, that flat was empty. His parents decided neither sell it nor let it, so I did not expect to be in trouble going there on our own. At first I reckoned maybe it would be a good idea to contact them before going to his flat, but I knew it was all too weird and I was not in the mood so as to be telling his parents about her, those gifts, the letter. I thought better of it, and came to realize the best I could do would be, well, taking her to there and find out what all of that was about.

*Are you sure you wanna enter?* I asked her right in front of that door. She did not respond, just nodded. *Okay then, let's go inside.* Saying this, I used the key and the door opened. Letting it ajar, we came in. A nasty odour welcomed us. An odour of something rotting. It is funny, at the time I got such a feeling: my soul was the culprit, my soul *was* that thing rotting, and thus I feared something wrong was about to happen to me. *You OKAY?* I heard her asking me. *Sure,* I responded, and so we both started looking around trying to discover where those gifts were.

3

As far as I can recall, the first time he told me about her was ten years ago. Back then, he was eager and excited each time he was talking to me about how they had met, when, where and what had happened at that very instant. It was the first time I saw him smiling openly, that's for sure. So, at his flat, while looking for those gifts, I paid much attention to her; how she leaned over to check some place out; what she wored; what she smelled of; how her large black hair felt down over her shoulders after each jerk. I was truly mystified about the sort of relationship they had had. It seemed unthinkable to me imaging these two having sex; or being at a gig, or whatever plans normally involved a couple of lovers. No; I knew then, and I think I know now, that my friend never touched her. According to that thought, I watched her moving around the flat, looking here and there, as if that one was the first time she was right there. She was a stranger. So was I.

*Over here,* she screamed, waving at me. I reached her and I saw an opened drawer, quite huge, containing some boxes. They looked like gifts, indeed. We picked them up, and put them on the dining room table. There were a total amount of four boxes, more or less looking the same. *Well, that's it. There, open them,* I said to her. She looked at me horrified, and I could understand why. Until then, we were more or less merely spectators, some sort of audience attending some

6

bizarre event, but then, inside that flat with all those boxes around, we knew we were about to take part in it.

*I love her,* I recalled he told me some years ago, while having dinner I can barely remember where. *I really do.* That had to be true, I think. Yes; she froze in front of those boxes, trying to make such a decision. I stared at her, trying to make a move but not being capable of. *What do I do now?,* she asked. *I dunno,* I think I answered, mumbling. It was obvious: she had to open all those boxes. But there was something impeding her from doing that, and whatever it was that thing, it was impeding me from making her to do that, indeed.

He travelled a lot while being alive. The first place he went was London; then he decided to pay Prague a visit. Each time he came back, he brought some kind of gift for all of us. Something for his mama, something for his papa, something for me, and, of course, something for *her.* What I had never come to realize was that all of those gifts were hidden in his flat, inside a drawer, well-preserved, but untouched. And not to mention the mere idea of knowing that, as a matter of fact, what he felt inside was quite different from what she felt inside, so I could at that very moment understand why he killed himself, after all. It was a matter of not being loved, I was positive about that theory. *I love her too much. I mean it. I really do.* Yeah, he did. Those four boxes were placed on that table, awaiting us to do something. She picked one and studied it intensively. It was a common box. *Go ahead, open it,* I encouraged her. She looked at me as if she realized I was there for the first time, and then her gaze went back to that box she was holding. *Okay, I will.*

It was a gift from London. A red telephone booth.

I'm not sure at all, but maybe we both were waiting for something really special to happen, I don't know what, and seeing that so-common red telephone booth, that friend of mine, somehow, had let us down.

The rest of those gifts turned out to be more or less the same, just some kinda sort of foolish things coming from different foreign countries. She looked tired and disappointed. *And is that all?,* she said to no one in particular. *I fear it is so, yes.*

4

I told you all; he was a stranger. She left the gifts where they were, and got out without looking back. I let her go. I stared for a while at those foolish things he bought somewhere, sometime, and I tried to think what they had meant to him, how he had chosen them all, and why. For he had decided to buy them for some reason, some reason I didn't even understand. I could even

7

imagine him buying them in some kind of shop, smiling while doing so, thinking about the day he would be able to give them to her. I could see that anxiety of his, that odd feeling of being in love, and that made me sick.

I tossed all those gifts back inside that drawer. I got out of the flat, shutting the door behind me. Then, I locked it using the key I still had. I went downstairs, until I could reach the street. It was still raining, and it was cold and windy. I walked for a while, thinking, getting wet. I didn't care. After a couple of minutes, I picked that key up from my pocket and gazed at it intensely. Finally, I threw it out, not even worrying where it landed, in case it did.

# MUM COMES HOME TWICE A WEEK

*"No live organism can continue for long
to exist sanely under conditions of absolute reality."*

Shirley Jackson, The Haunting Of Hill House

*To Esther: go for it!*
*To Pilar: thanks for reading my first try in English.*
*To Jos: my first English teacher who had become an actual friend.*
*To my friends & parents & relatives: thanks for being there all the time.*

1

"Mum comes home twice a week", said the girl, looking out the window, where a frozen little orchard could be seen, "and, when she does, she expects from me to be *'ere*." She was elegantly seated on a wooden stool, her back turned on him. Beside her, a huge hearth was spreading warmth all across the drawing room, darkened enough because of the dusk. He stood on his feet, staring at her silently, trying to make out those uttered words, mystified. "Thus, I have to be *'ere* twice a week, accordingly. You see?", added the girl, turning her head delicately in order to look deeply inside his eyes.

Oh, sweet creature! He nodded, smiling. That part of the house was odd, but somehow cosy. It was a small room, and being so he wondered for such a long time about what sort of suitors had been waiting as he had, or even what amount of them had been keeping that same chat concerning her mother visits whilst looking at those frozen dead trees, in that decrepit orchard where no fruits seemed to be produced any more. How many? One? Two? Oh, he thought, surely a huge quantity. She was a pretty dark horse, the kind of girl whom one could sickly fall in love with; the one having all the enigmas and the minimal oddities so as to become, let's say, almost perfect and seldom found. Quite so, he wanted to be engaged to her.

She smiled back at him. Her eyes glowed of pure intensity. "Then, if you want to date me during those visits, you have to come over before or after my mum comes, obviously." She got up and walked to and fro, trying not to touch him, "Oh, I guess mum's not going to care about that."

9

Outside, it started to snow slightly. The frozen orchard was whitened, so it was not noticeable if it had not been for the footpath leading to the front door, covered with pebbles, almost as if it was a shingle beach, was getting as white as the orchard. "I love the snow", said she. "Why's that?", it was his first question after entering the house. "Oh, it is depressing. It makes me think about long journeys ending in lovers meeting." He stared at her and said: "Quite so, indeed."

So, the night fell down and he could see the orchard no more. She moved quickly to the other side of the drawing room, where a small pile of logs waited, patiently, to be chosen. She picked two or three up, and hurled them to the hearth. A few sparks announced the fire was not going to cease. "There," she said smoothly, " I think it is warm enough in 'ere. Mum is going to be comfortable when she arrives." She waited in front of the hearth, her face illuminated by the dim light of the drawing room, concealing her hands inside her dressing gown pockets. "I love the fire, as well", she muttered. He reached her and put his right hand over her left shoulder, standing his ground behind her. He felt the pleasant smoothness of her delicate dressing gown's material. She did not move at all, so he dared to say: "I'm going to wait for your mother, if you want." To that, she moved away, provoking his right hand to float in the air, as if missing something which had never been there before. "I don't think it's a good idea, my dear", she noted, "Mum is terribly shy, and she does not want strangers in her house." He pondered for the best part of a minute. Eventually, he said: "I can understand that, of course. But surely I am not a stranger, or am I?" She came to him, again, and  caressed his face with her fingertips: "Yes, you *are*, indeed", she approached him a little more, her perfume drowsing his senses, "My beloved sweet stranger." He closed his eyes for a bit, trying to focus. That odour was penetrating his nostrils quite violently. "Sure, maybe you are my own stranger, ready to satisfy me whenever I am in need.", she said, brutally, whilst looking at him intently. "Mum is jealous, as well", she added, evilly. He opened his eyes, pulling himself together in order to resist that fragrance weakening him completely, and came to say: "Is she jealous because of me?" She laughed: "I guess not", she separated herself from him, turning around and went by the stool, where she was seated some minutes ago: "She loves me desperately." She looked through the window, letting her gaze be mixed with the darkness outside: "I don't want you here when she gets home." Then, sitting on the stool, she ended: "It wouldn't be safe." He was startled, looking at her silhouetted figure seated on that stool, placed opposite the window, and said: "I'm not scared of your mother. I could not be."

She smiled widely. The darkness outside was complete, and the silence was only altered by some logs crackling by the fire in the hearth. "Oh, you are not he first one talking nonsense, my dear", she said sadly. "All the same, I don't want you 'ere and that's all."

He came closer, placing himself between the window and the stool. Then, looking down at her pretty and sad face, he tried to find out what sort of enigmatic dilemmas she had in mind, if so, and how to decipher them. "You know I love you, don't you?", he inquired hastily. "Yes, indeed", was her quick response. "Then, why should I be afraid of your mother?" She looked up, a single tear rolling down her left cheek: "It's the way it has to be", she answered. "I cannot understand that", he admitted, tiredly, "now, who's talking nonsense?", he concluded.

It was late at night. The only way to go back to the city was by car, and certainly he was aware of driving frozen roads in the night. "I cannot go, not now", he said. "Indeed, it is dangerous", she admitted trying to peer through the window: "You cannot leave now, that's for sure." Then, he grabbed her by her shoulders and, with a jerk, made her get up all of a sudden. Their eyes met for a second, and he could feel her entire body trembling. "I love you", he muttered. Behind her, a crack was heard, another log being consumed by the fire. "I love you", he repeated, looking at her intently, craving for a response. "I love you too", she finally said, and their lips became one for a quantum, and her body relaxed and the drawing room melt down, like ice, and all was fine. "Let me stay", he implored, eagerly, drawing his head back to gaze at her, " I beg you." She shocked her head hesitantly, and ascertained to say: "There's no way." So, he put her away and went by the hearth, and observing the logs burning down to ashes, he asked: "Why don't you want me to stay by your side?". Somewhere, he heard a car's engine, so far away, "Why?". She stood where she was, trembling again. She felt very sorry for him: "My mum", she responded, as if that was the real matter of it all, "I don't think it is a good idea, anyway." "Nonsense!", he screamed. He turned around and looked at her; she barely saw him clearly because he was standing right in front of the fire, so to her he was merely a sombre. "As you said, I cannot leave now", he pointed out. "Yes," she admitted dryly, " you have to stay. It is such a paradox, isn't it?", she asked out of the blue, somehow amused. "Thus, you have to hide", she came to such a realization in no time. "Hide?". "Yes, my dear," she continued, " you have to hide 'ere, maybe below my bed or inside some closet." He burst into laughs. "You're mocking me!" She looked daggers at him: "I'm dead serious", she said angrily. "You cannot stay freely whilst my mum is 'ere. It is not safe." He stopped laughing. "You *are* serious!", she shrugged, "for God's sake. Who the hell is your mum?". She smiled at him, and took his hands with hers and drove him by the window. "You don't want to know", she answered, dryly. "She is all I have, and I am all she has, as well. It is fair to say we have each other, you see", he was astonished. "Let me put you in some place where she cannot find you." "What if she does?", he asked nervously. She did not answer. "I'm getting scared, I think", he said almost in a whisper. "Hush!," said she, " you are going to be okay, trust me." So, she took him from one room to another: from the dinning room to the bathroom; from the bathroom to the bedroom, from there to a lot of huge and creepy closets; from those not quite comfortable closets to some sort

11

of weird and unnamed rooms full of odd and unknown stuff, and not having find the best and safest place to stay, and knowing her mother was going to be there in no time, she eventually came to a bright idea: "Wait!," she shouted suddenly, giving him the chills, "you can go spend the night inside your car!". He nodded, "that's pretty much what I ascertain as a good idea", he admitted. "And besides, my mum could see the car during the morning. So, you'll be better going as soon as the sun is shining", he added cleverly. He nodded again: "I know."

Thus, he got out of the house and hurried to the car. It was freezing out there, and he trudged in order to get to the car without falling down on that slippery ground. He passed across that frozen orchard, looking at the dead trees and the dead frozen soil. From there, he could see her silhouetted through the drawing room window, the only warm place in all that huge household. He got in the car and, closing the door, adjusted the car windows accordingly, impeding the slightest cold air from getting in. "What now?", he thought, still looking in her direction, "she is staring at me", he was sure of it. "And she loves me, she has to", he said to himself, feeling sleepy and, indeed, falling asleep in some moment during that agitated creepy cold winter night. Whilst he was dozing, she went to the dining room and waited there for two hours. At three o'clock, the front door's latch moved slightly.

"Mum, is that you?"

2

"Honestly, I don't know what to think", he said. The cold of the last winter night was over and, despite the fact the weather was as hard as ever, he could appreciate the smoothness of some sun rays caressing his skin. One of those best friends of his was looking at him through an intense cloud made of cigar smoke. Surrounding them, a pleasant collection of tall and ancient trees, now dead because of the winter, but still looking pleasant; a pack of benches here and there, some of them empty and some others full of seated people immersed in some sort of gay chats; "No," he thought, "this is a bright day in spite of the cold and the winter, so *that* did not take place." That friend of his looked worried, and determined to last his cigar for ages, he observed it largely. Then, he said: "It's odd, it is, indeed", to that he sighed: "I got out of there at sunrise, as I was told",  his friend put his gaze  away from the cigar for a bit and looked at him, puzzled: "So?" "So," he explained, "I came home pretty early in the morning." "Didn't you see her?", asked his friend, frowning. "Nope." "As I said, weird, so weird, indeed." That smoke coming out from that splendid cigar seemed to cover them completely, as if trying to make them invisible. "You need to forget all about her, old chap", pointed out his friend, "It seems to me this is not going to do any good to you." He nodded, almost absently. Some paces afar, a child was playing with a black ball. His mother was comfortably seated on a bench opposite him, reading *The Picture of Dorian Gray*. She was beautiful, as beautiful as almost her beloved, he thought, and her delicate neck was protected from the cold by a woollen red scarf. From time to time, she looked up, put her book aside, upon the bench, marking carefully the last read page using a bookmark, and kept an eye on her son. "Be careful, sweetheart", she said sometime, "Don't! Don't!", she said later on, "Now, that's quite rude to do!", she screamed once, and "Don't make me get up!", said she crossed enough, looking daggers at her almost scared son. He smiled. "Why, it is only a child. Don't be so rough", he said in a whisper. "What?", asked his friend, looking at him. "Never mind", he responded. "So," started his friend again, "what are you going to do?" "'bout what?", he asked back. "Why, 'bout her, obviously", shouted that friend of his, quite astonished. "Oh, I don't know yet. Maybe I'm going to pay her a visit tomorrow evening, her mother is not going to be there, I guess." So, his friend shocked his head violently, and said: "No, you are not." The kid was crying. Something had happened to him whilst he was distracted talking to his friend. His mother got up hastily, and put herself beside her son trying to determine what was, in fact, wrong. "What have you done?", she asked, dusting his pants. "Fool!", she screamed, angrily. "How awful!", she added, putting an exceptional effort in cleaning the poor kid's trousers from dust, mud and some glued snow. "I beg your pardon?", asked his friend. "Don't make a fool of yourself, *goddammit!*", said he. "You cannot go back there, that would be pointless. Go look for another pretty face elsewhere!", his cigar was almost done. "She's more than a pretty face, you know." "It does not matter: she is a dark horse, you said so. I don't like dark horses among me and the friends of mine." He laughed: "No, of course you don't."

He looked back at that mother and her son. The child was done with the crying, but her mother was talking to him down. At least, he thought, she is not screaming, any more. The book she left upon the bench was opened by some undetermined page, and a cold wind coming all of a sudden paged the book to and fro, as if some supernatural entity was trying to read the book chaotically, in such an extravagant order. "Let's go home this instant," said the mother, "it's getting windy." And then, they disappeared somewhere behind a pack of frozen white dead bushes. "You see," said he, "I would like to be that kid's father." "How awful!", shouted his friend, looking at him scared. "You surely don't want *that*!", and then continued as if explaining an obvious universal truth to such an slow student in some *a-long-time-ago* forsaken classroom, "to be engaged is to be dead, my friend", he frowned. "Don't look at me like that, you know I am right." "No, I don't." That wind breezed again, and he decided it was the right time to come back home. "That woman was not mistaken at all: it is getting awfully windy." "So, what?", asked his friend. "So, I'm making a move home. You come?" His friend seemed to ponder for a bit, then responded: "Sure, my cigar's done.

There's nothing here for me, any more." They got up and started to walk out the gardens.

He looked back. He thought it was really odd to see that bench empty, not even five seconds right after getting up from there, and now it looked at him absent, simply wooden material, painted brown, put there in order to be useful, alone if it were not for the others, more or less looking the same, accompanying it, absolutely unconcerned. And what about that bench, some paces away, where that mother had been seated reading her book? Empty, as well. "Look," said he to his friend, pointing at some further distance. "What is it?" "There's nothing there. Just emptiness." That friend of his, looking puzzled, said finally: "Why, old chap, I guess you are as odd as that *fiancé* of yours."

But I am right, he thought, because there was no one else in those gardens. The latest human being presence was finally over, and now the dead trees and the frozen white bushes, among the painted brown benches, were the only creatures dwelling there.

3

"She says beauty is a stationary state," her words were spoken calmly, clearly. The fireplace was still offering warmth and cosiness, as the logs were crackling and burning down, inside that ancient mammoth house, "so, I *am* a stationary beauty, you see." "Oh, we are all such stationary beings, that's for sure", said he. "She is fond of me," she added quite suddenly, "because of that." He could not understand that. "Why?", he asked her. "She is getting on a bit, she is tired and somehow exhausted and she thinks she is not worthy any more", she confessed, sadly, looking at the back of her hands: "Look," she said, lifting them both, "can you see it?" "I don't know what you mean", he admitted, mystified. She smiled and put her hands down. "I guess you are like the others." She came forth, where she could survey him deeply. "What do you want from me?", asked he. "It's not what I want, but what *mum* wants. She's got *rules*."

A knock came to the front door quite suddenly. She turned back, startled. "Who could that be?", she asked herself, and left the drawing room smoothly. He stood his ground, almost paralysed. He did not dare to make a move, but he could hear her talking. "To whom?", he thought. "Look, it is not even dark." "It can't be her mum, she said..." The front door was shut. She came back, showing a sad expression of extreme disgust. "Well, is anything wrong?", he asked. "Not sure", she responded, looking down at the floor, as if seeking for something. "Well, who was it?", he tried again, hopeless. "Oh," she lift her head a bit, " it was a police officer." He shuddered. "What? Why?", he demanded to know. "Oh, that's something I cannot tell." "For God's sake!", he exclaimed, staring at her a bit suspicious. "Does it have anything to do with your mother?" "You dare!", she blasted, "Don't talk about my mum like that!" She went by the wooden stool, in front of

14

the sole drawing room window, and sat down. "She's got rules, as I said. That is all." He came closer, and knelt on the tiled floor, right in front of her. He put his hands upon her knees. "I'm so sorry, darling. I didn't mean...." "Oh, it is okay, you could not know." She smiled at him. "Tell me all about those rules of hers, I want to know." She put her own hands upon his, so the effect was quite dramatic. "I love you", she said, strangely. "Oh, but I *do* know that." "But still," she whispered, " I had to say it." He got up and taking her hands drove her closer to the hearth. A frugal kiss was intended, but she unfolded her arms and pushed him away. "Don't", she said. He tried again, this time she revealed to be stronger. "What's wrong?", he asked. "Mum is not going to tolerate such a behaviour in her own house." "What the...!", he shouted, loudly. "She's got rules. She said so when she arrived 'ere and she *smelled* you." He was totally astonished. He let his arms fell down, suspended, supported only by his own shoulders, with his fingers touching the void, his skin feeling the warmth sprat out by the hearth, right behind him. "She said I should take care of myself as long as you were 'ere."

*Rules.* How odd! Rules and cosy fireplaces where one could feel that stationary beauty talking nonsense. "Tell me, then, what those rules are all about", he implored. "I beg you, I want to know. I need to know. I have to." She grinned: "I guess you are going to hate them." He took a deep breath and said: "I'll avoid speaking mind, I promise." She put a straight face and kissed him in the forehead. "You're so sweet, my dear." Then, she walked some paces away, turning her back on him and looked outside through that sole window, unaware of the darkness. "So be it", she added.

4

There was an empty cup all by itself upon the round marbled table of the *café*. Seated at it, he was peering inside that cup quite intently. Apart from the yellow-coloured ceramic bottom, he could see no more. Inside, the snugness, the almost childish sensation he was perfectly safe among all those who, like him, were having coffees and chats, and laughs and cries, and hopes and desires. A waiter came, carrying another cup of coffee. He put it upon the table using his left hand, whilst taking the other with his right. "Anything else?", the waiter asked. "No, I'm fine, thanks." No; he was not: he brushed away an imaginary strand of hair over his forehead, and sipped some more coffee from that new this time green-coloured ceramic cup. "*Hey*, old chap!" he heard out of the blue, and turning his head around he could see his friend, smiling, taking a seat in front of him. "So, how are you doing?" He left a book upon the table, before him. It was in a bad condition, meaning it was read thousands of times. Its cover had such a lack of colour, depicting an ancient ghastly manor, surrounded by high hills almost fainted because of a pale-yellowish dense mist. Some dark tree branches were embracing the house. "Oh, old chap, you look so pale!", said his friend. "What happened last night?", he wanted to know. "She told me *things*." "Well, what things could these possibly be?" He left the cup upon the table, empty. "You are not going to believe me", he added, dryly. "Try me." Another waiter came, not carrying anything, and asked his friend what it would be. "Oh, I'll have a black coffee, please." The waiter bowed, and vanished almost instantly, only to reappear after a few seconds with a hot pink-coloured ceramic cup, this time bigger than the ones containing just coffee, and put it upon the table, right in front of him, beside that second hand book. "There you are, sir." "Thank you", said he, and then, having a sip from it he turned his face directly towards him, and added: "now, it is time for you to tell me all about those creepy things she filled you in. I'm all ears."

Winter, cold, and loneliness. That could perfectly be such a fair description of that mysterious girl he was in love with. He spent some minutes trying to find the words in order to explain, plainly, what he was told that last night, avoiding explicitly to miss some important and conclusive stuff. Then, he started talking: "There are three rules I have to know, and obey", he caressed his empty cup of coffee with his forefinger's tip, "The first one applies to the house by itself: I am not allowed to be in another room but the drawing room, that restriction not including the obvious fact I have to pass through some others in order to reach it. Her mother calls those rooms as *the inner ones*." His friend looked at him amused. "Now, what a foolish rule to make up!", he commented, smiling. "The second one," he continued, " is about sex. It is not I cannot have sex with her daughter, that is not the point. This second rule accepts sex as a whole, but I cannot have sex with her *inside* the house. Not even a hug, not to mention a kiss." His friend grinned quite diabolically and said: "Chap, you have to take her away from that old chilly house for sure, if you don't want to be pleasuring yourself till the end of times!" He nodded slowly. Then, the same waiter as before came back and asked them if they were fine. His friend asked for a new cup of black coffee. The waiter bowed, again, and vanished. They both waited till the black coffee, this time in a pale-white ceramic cup, was left upon the table, to go along with the last and incredible rule: "The third one is even much odder: I am not allowed, by all means, to meet her mother. Ever." His friend applauded noisily, and barked: "Yeah! I *love* this one!" Some customers looked at them, unnapprovingly. "Stop the clapping, would you?", asked him. He was in two minds about that mysterious girl. When they met, some months ago, she looked as enigmatic as ever, but still he fell in love with her almost immediately. One day, they went out for a walk, during the autumn season. The woodland was gorgeous, leaves falling down their trees, in quite a different colour-tones of brown, yellow, and nuclear red. Their feet stepped over a smooth layer of dead but still colourful bed of leaves. It was then when she admitted she would like to own a small flat in the city, where she could go to bookshops and cafés, and where she could talk to everyone she wanted to. She started describing what kind of flat she was thinking of, and he smiled because it seemed quite apart from that enormous house she lived in. "It would be a small place, with a huge library where myriads of books telling about a pile of varying subjects would dwell; so I would arrive tired of being all day long working hard, and I would relax myself laying down in the sofa, letting my gaze to be lost amidst all those shelves and books they would contain in..." He hugged her, then it was correct to do so, he thought, and she smiled back and kissed him and started to run and played hide and seek for a while. "You would be always welcome in my little place, and we could stare at my library together, and fall asleep and wake up in the middle of the night and make love and whisper to one another: *I love you, I love you...*" Then he understood she had been alone, she had always been alone, but the real motive was far from being ascertained, and when they were pretty tired of being outdoors, they bade their goodbyes, and he left her there, getting in his car and droving off.

"She would like to own a small flat," said he to his friend, " a very small flat, indeed." He could see her sad face through the veil of darkness he was in. "Every morning, I would fix some coffee in my kitchen, listening to the latest news on the radio, and letting my imagination fly away, away, and I would pay no attention to the world I would be in, except when that would suite me, so I would be as happy as ever, and I would call you whenever I needed you, and you would touch my face with your fingertips, and I would suppress a scream of ecstasy, for I would not like to be notorious as a consequence of being in the dirty awful mouths of all those noisy neighbours." "What's your life like?", he asked her some other day, whilst having a coffee in that cosy drawing room, this time it was summer so they kept the window opened. "Pleasant", he responded mechanically. "Oh, I see, don't you want to tell me?" "It is not so, my dear", she said, smiling, "But I'd rather tell you all about the book I'm reading now." He knew she was keen on literature, so it was almost impossible not to fall in love with her: he was as passionate as she was concerning books. "I see, tell me then, what is your book about?" Her eyes glowed. "It's about an apparently weak girl trying to find her own way to be happy, in an old creepy house like this one", she pointed at the hearth, "It has a huge fireplace, and a lot of different rooms and weird stuff, and at least I could count three varying supernatural manifestations occurring in there." He felt a cold breeze caressing his backbone. Back in the café, he grabbed his friend's book and looked directly at its cover. *The Haunting Of Hill House,* was its title. "What a curious coincidence!", he exclaimed, tapping at the book's cover. "What is it, old chap?", asked his friend, intrigued. "She read the same book." "Oh, but I don't even start the reading, you know. I just carry it with me because I intent to read it *soon*." He handed the book to his friend, nodding. "It *is* a second hand book, is it not?, he wanted to know. "Sure. Cheaper, you know."

"In the book," he recalled her elaborating, "this girl died, but somehow she found that way to an absolute deep happiness she was in search for. It is not always right there, in some exact place you could trace, or locate, in a map, or just think of because you know it is real."

"Who is her mum, anyway?", asked his friend, saving the book inside a bag which was barely unfolded to allow the book to fit in. "I don't know." His friend moved slightly on that chair. "Well, you'll better know. Or maybe you have to get her out of that house, if you really think you love her." He was in doubt. "It is uncommon to find a mother like this one, I guess", he admitted. "But still, it is her daughter, and I am not sure she is going to come with me. I fear she is not", said he, miserably. "Don't lose your head, old chap." "I am not sure what to do, it is complicated." All around them, the café was getting empty from the customers were leaving the place. Her smile was present in his mind, and her fragrance and her pose. It was an impressive pose, indeed, and the mere thought of her pretty sad face holding his gaze, late that night, whilst explaining those rules, feeling she was somehow devastated doing so, almost perceiving a tear not wanting to roll down her cheek, made him depressed, hopeless, terrified. He could go, kidnap her, put her away from that old creepy household and her enigmatic mother, and then, what? Was she going to hate him for what he could possibly do, or maybe was she going to love him deeply because of that? "Look there, my sweet stranger," she said on one such occasion, in that manor of hers, pointing at what looked like an old small graveyard, "there all my family lay down." He thought *that* was scary, and he asked politely why she was revealing to him that small empty place where surely only the dead would dwell for ages even when they both were purely dust and memories of the past. "Why, because it *is* what is left of my family." And she gazed at it, as if contemplating the brightest stars in a black cloudless sky at night.

"I guess tomorrow night her mother is going to come over", he said. "Yeah, *mum comes home twice a week*, I got it", said his friend, amused. "So, I guess I'm going." "Excuse me?" "I said I guess I *am* going", repeated he. "Yes," said after a while, more convinced, "I made up my mind, I'm truly determined to go and talk to her mother. That's it." His friend moved again on that chair, showing him he was starting to get tired of being seated there. "But she said... the third rule..." He cut him off quickly: "Stop that, mate. She is just a mother, and I can even understand her and those odd rules she told me about. See...", he paused for a bit, trying to find the words which could suite that explanation the best, "She told me once she would like to own a small flat and to be there on her own. She would be happy. At that time I thought she was exaggerating, but now I know I do understand her." He looked resolute enough to his friend's eyes. "I am going to get her out of that old house, but I am going to do things properly." "Okay, then, tell me: what are you up to?"

For the best part of a minute, he said nothing. The café was, by now, deserted. They were the only customers. In some place inside that café, they could hear noises coming from crockery, cutlery and chinas being carried. Finally, he said evilly: "Didn't you figure it out yet? I'm going to break those sick rules, all of them, one after another, *systematically*."

5

It was hot in *there*. The logs were still crackling in the hearth, and she was seated on that wooden stool. There was no one accompanying her lonely solitude, otherwise that odd gaze she was holding would have been widely commented for years to come; but she was *alone*, and therefore she could drift her gaze elsewhere: not at the cosy drawing room where she prefered to spend all day long; not at the fireplace, where a beam of light coming out from the hearth was illuminating briefly her pale pretty sad face; not even at the frozen orchard out there, right behind that sole huge window, now almost imperceptible because of the darkness and the mist; not here or there, but *beyond*. "Don't cry, sweetheart," she could hear her mum saying, back in time, in that weird beyond belonging to that happy past, "here's your mum." She cuddled her, put some kisses on her forehead, and embraced her tight, and whispered some sweet words and she calmed down, and she opened her eyes and looked at her mum and smiled, and her mum looked down at her and smiled back, and kept hugging her for a while, until she could stop that awful crying and wiped her eyes and stoped shivering. "He is not worthy of you, my dear." And she was pretty sure of that that instant, just because it was something coming out from *her mum*. Outside, somewhere amidst that dark moor, far from reach, she could discern some sort of a lament, probably human. The old huge and chilly household was located in the outskirts of that not quite big city, standing over its own walls, emerging from the soil like a summoned creature. There they lived in peace, in spite of that sick atmosphere and cold air, where even during the summer nights an additional blanket was truly required in order to avoid some chills. Memories, remembrances of that lovely past even when she got hurt, during that unforgettable and unforgivable episode, when she was excessively young and naïve and did not understand a clue about men. She felt in love, obvious thing to do when one is young and beauty, splendid, an actual blossom during the spring. Thus, her mother observed her from the distance only a mother could cope with; when she got home at night, she was questioned every now and again about what kind of suitor he was, what things they used to do together, if he was touching her *down there*, and if so, if she was feeling something new and dirty. But she said no all the times, trying to put her mother's thoughts and worries at rest, and so her mum was tranquil for a while, at least during the few hours preceding the next date. It was painful when it came, all of a sudden: she came home crying miserably, all her make-up fucked up, buring her face inside the

19

back of her two hands, making breathless noises and hurrying upstairs, until she reached her bedroom and there she stood, slaming the door behind her, hurling herself upon the bed. Her mum was downstairs, looking up and letting her anger flaring, unstoppable. "He dared!", she shouted, angrily, "He dared!".

It came to happen that that suitor was trying to demonstrate he was not queer. Clever but always alone, all the gossip was involved in his hypothetical homosexuality. Therefore, he got a girlfriend and was sure of showing up himself all the time attached to her, kissing her smooth and red innocent lips in public, holding her tight and smiling enamoured at her. She met his parents, his most important and beloved friends and relatives, and she spent some time dinning at their tables and small flats, having chats and talking about the most diverse subjects. She felt she belonged, at last, *there*. His flat was small, indeed, but full of books. Here, there and everywhere she could find tall shelves containing a huge impressive collection of books talking philosophy and philology. Among others, she found *Plato's The Republic*, the complete works of *Heideger* in German, obviously, and *A La Reserche du Temps Perdu*, written by *Proust*, in such a colourful French. She was impressed, and so she came to love him *deeply*. Thus, she felt betrayed and miserable when the awful truth came forth: it was there, in that same small place, that in killing some time, she said to him she would be proud of introducing him to her marvellous and beloved mother, and maybe they could, from that moment on, begin planning their wedding. That came to happen one dull October morning. He was reading in the sitting room *Henry Jame's The Turn Of The Screw. Dark Sanctuary* was on the cd-player, some huge clock on the wall was ticking desperately. "I said...", she started over. He sighed and put the book aside, upon the settee he was seated on, and stared at her coldly. "I am not interested", was all he said dryly. "But I thought ..." At that, he extended his left arm and showing the back of his left hand directly to her face, he concluded: "Now, all my relatives and friends know I am not queer; thus, I am not going to need anything from you, any more. You are due to get away. Now, if you'd please...", and, having said that, he picked up the book from the settee and resumed his reading, not paying attention to her. Thus, he did not see her silent cry, her total disappointment and sadness and sorrow, and so, he could not see how she went away, running, and how she got home and her mother looked at her hitting the roof.

"Where are you now, mother?", she asked no one in particular. The stress was closing in; she could feel it. It was pitch black out there, so she could see, now that she came back to that reality, her reflection painted faintly on the window. For a bit, she could not recognize her own face, and she got scared of her own reflection within that accidental mirror. Then, she smiled and got up from the stool and approached the hearth. Tomorrow evening my mum will be here, she thought. Oh, good God! That was relief, somehow. After all that misery she had been through, after all the sadness and the angriness and the coldness, now she was free to be with her mum, at least twice a week, and so her heart was at ease, and she could wake up every morning and do things easily, like cleaning up the entire house and taking care of absolutely everything, just in order to avoid letting her mother down. She loved her with all her heart. She was the sole friend she got, the only one understanding her feelings completely, the only not trying to take her away, far away, from all that once had belonged to her, like this old creepy house. That night she went to bed happily, eagerly even, craving for the next day to come. Whilst sleeping, lying down in the bed, covered with two layers of blankets, put them there just upon some white bedlinen, smelling of flowers and sweets, she dreamt pleasantly, a wide smile deforming her yet still red and innocent lips, but just slightly.

Far from that house, he was staring at the ceiling, incapable of resting. Upon his face, a weird mixture of eagerness and regretfulness, as if trying to determine which one was going to win that interior argument, if that could be even feasible. The bedroom was darkened. He could see what time it was thanks to a red-bright alarm clock digital display, which was resting upon a small bed-table. Its intense mercury-coloured light-beam could be follow, slightly, with the corners of his eyes. It was cold out there, but the central heating he decided to install yesteryear coped with that quite successfully, so he could not feel any cold in there. He knew it was late, but he could barely sleep. As soon as he closed his eyes, he saw her in that house. "Wait for me, my darling," he said in a loud voice, "I'm coming."

6

"I told you not to come over," she said, crossed. He shrugged and asked her permission to get in. It started to snow violently that evening, so some snowflakes lied upon his leather coat-shoulders, and his scarf was whitened despite the fact red used to be its colour. "It is freezing, may I come in?" She looked impatient. "Of course, otherwise you will perish out there." She let him in, sparing some room in order to allow him to pass her without touching her. "Do me a favour, and stay in the drawing room, would you?" He was going towards that room, indeed. Whilst doing so, he nodded. She shut the door. The floor by the doorway was a bit wet. She made a move to the drawing room following him, who was taking his leather coat off. He put it upon the stool. Dusting his scarf from snowflakes, he said: "I wanted to see you." She approached him from behind, her cheeks reddened as a consequence of that comfortable fire spreading warmth. She embraced him and let her head rest, for a while, against his back. "I love you so much," she said in a whisper, "but I told you not to come over when my mum..." she paused, sighing. There was only a forced silence, jeopardized from time to time by the crackling of those burning logs in the hearth. He waited for her to continue. Finally, she did: "I'd rather want you to be far away." "Why's that?", he asked politely. "I want to know." She went away from him quite suddenly. "You know the rules, I told you." "Yes, you did, indeed. But still." She smiled slightly; there he was: the first suitor who did love her, probably the only one she would ever meet, and between them those unfair rules. What if she decided to have sex with him that instant? She was excited, indeed; it would be easy to hurl herself upon his powerful arms and cover his face with passionate endless kisses. She felt an intense spark of flames down there, right in the groin, and put her hands over the wall, at one side of the window, as if preventing herself from putting them elsewhere. "You could be with me, you know that, do you not?", he asked her. "Where?" "Somewhere else." "But, what would I do in that *somewhere else* place?" "Not much." "Be happy?" "Perhaps." "With you?" "With me." "For years to come?" "For ever." "And shall we be happy always?" "I promise." "Always?" "Always." She went by his side, looking at his eyes deeply. He took her hands and kissed them both delicately. She closed her eyes and let him caressed her face using his fingertips, and then a sole tear showed up. He wiped it away with one finger, and kissed her in the mouth. Those yet still red innocent lips opened automatically, allowing his tongue to get in and search for hers, deeply buried inside that wet cavity. When they met, she felt an intense spasm and her legs weakened, thus she almost fell down if it had not been for those powerful arms of his, holding her tightly. "I cannot do this", she complained, mumbling. He looked at her mystified. "Who are you, sweet creature?" "No one", she responded, still keeping her eyes shut. "Let me save you, please", he implored, almost crying. "What for?" "I love you." "That's not enough, I fear." "It has to be." "No, it never has to." She opened her eyes: now she was crying silently but he could discern her spasms and trembling, aroused. "Let's go upstairs,", she said. "What about your mother?" "We still have some time." "I don't want to hurry." She opened her eyes and smiled oddly. "Come," and grabbed his left hand and led him upstairs, leaving the drawing room behind. That part of the house was surrounded by weird shadows. It was cold, probably because there was no central heating at all, so not wearing his leather coat he was terribly cold despite the sexual arouse he was experiencing, and therefore he commited her to hurry upstairs, until finding quite a shelter down the woollen brown blankets of her bed. The bedroom was a small one. Through those shadows painted oddly on the walls, he could make out a simple lamp upon a wooden small bed-table, and opposite the bed, where they were now lying in, a huge ancient wardrobe seemed to be watching them. In her naked embrace, he felt her smooth skin and her warmth, and he could contain his own excitement no more. So, amidst that terrible blizzard, they made love, and he could hear some snowflakes hitting the bedroom window, and the hiss of the cold wind pushing them, and he could even hear uncommon noises and what he thought it was an afar lament, probably human, but being in that paradise of young delicate skin he thought about that no more, and thus he fell asleep against her naked and small body, whilst she toyed with some wild strands of dark hair glued to his forehead.

A shaking came about three o'clock: he woke up, a bit drowsy, hearing her panicking: "Wake up! Wake up!" He sat up, turning his head towards her, now a mere blurred image as a consequence of that drowsiness inherent to his dream; little by little, her face was being painted plainly, so at last he could appreciate her scared expression possessing her flaring eyes. She was moving her head quite violently, focussing on him for a while and on the bedroom door for a bit more. "What is it, my dear? What's wrong?", he asked, grabbing her face by putting his two hands on each cheek, determined to stop her convulsive movement. "Tell me!" She was totally gone. Her eyes could hardly look at him, and he managed to detect some sort of spasm provoking her entire body shivering noticeably. "Stop that!", he blasted at her, slapping her face. "What is it? What's going on!" She attained to say: "It's my mum! She's here, I heard the front door's latch moving!" He got up rapidly, leaving her upon the bed. "It's okay, I can go talk to her", he said, slowly, ensuring she could hear his words and understand them pretty well. He started to get dress, looking for his trousers and all around the bedroom. "No, you can't!", she shouted. "Stay here!" He got his trousers and was putting them on. "Don't be silly, my dear. I can handle this." She was still naked, so he could see some strands of hair falling delicately upon her generous breasts. He was aroused for a moment, but he put that sensation away quickly. "All is going to be fine, trust me", said he, heading towards the door. "Stay here! Don't go downstairs!", she spouted. He paid no attention to her, and opened the bedroom's door decidedly. The entire household was covered in shadows, and it was really cold there. He could not hear any sort of noise coming from the landing, downstairs. He made a move that way, his gaze fixed ahead. "Hello?" No answer. He continued going down, until he reached the first floor. To his left, there was the drawing room. The door was shut, and he could feel the warmth through it. "Hello? Ma'am, are you in there?", he asked, but no answer was given. He knocked at the door slightly, and waited for some response. Finally, he opened it and got inside. The drawing room was empty. Mystified, he turned back and got out, closing the door behind him. The kitchen was opposite, so he went towards it. This time, the door was ajar. "Ma'am, are you in here? I want to talk to you about your daughter." Before entering the kitchen, he peered across the gap left by the door. He saw nothing. "Hello?", he repeated. He was about to get in when out of the blue, her beloved's voice, upstairs, in the bedroom, said: "Don't mum, *don't*!" Shocked, he turned on his heels and went upstairs, as fast as he could, towards the bedroom. "I promise, mum, I promise!", he could hear her whining. "I'm going to be a good girl,don't, please, don't, *don't*!" He hurried up, he was almost there. "What's happening? *Hey*!", he screamed, pointlessly. Then, he heard a terrible sound of glasses being broken and an intense and creepy yell, fading away quickly. When he got in the bedroom, she was nowhere to be seen. There were scraps of glasses scattered all around the floor and the bed. "Darling! Darling!", he shouted, jumping over the bed, cutting himself with some of the glasses, not paying attention to that. "Where are you! My dear!" He bent over in order to see through that broken window. Myriad of snowflakes were getting in, now that there was no protection at all from the blizzard, and the bedroom was getting colder and colder every second. When he looked down, amidst the cold, the snow and the wind, he discerned what appeared to be a body, lying down in the ground, quiet. "No!", he now cried, "Oh, good God! No, no, it can't be!" The snow was whitening the bed by now, and the wind, fiercely, was hitting his face. "No, my God, no!", he exclaimed, all over again, looking down through that broken window, where she lied, dead. He rested there for a while, crying, calling her name aloud, whilst the snowflakes were covering the entire corpse of his beloved determinedly, little by little, until there, in that precise spot, only the snow could be seen.

# THE BOARDING HOUSE

*Despair is the source of all life*
*Self-Destruction the only way.*
*I choose death to live!*

**Dark Fortress, Stab Wounds.**

*Beyond a certain age, a journey across the city becomes uncomfortably reflective. The addresses of*
*the dead pile up.*

**Ian McEwan, Atonement.**

To Ida and Kees; they know why.

1

It is late at night; some people wander around quite drunk, avoiding explicitly to come close to the canal: they don't want to fall down, probably. It is a nice night, though: from time to time one can feel the warm wind slight touch right on the face; here and there friends go in bunches, laughing, passing by the boarding house doors, not even noticing it, just another house amidst the old medieval streets of the city. And besides, it is pitch black in there; no lights in the boarding house: just darkness and silence through its walls. Thus, how could anyone pay attention to it? All that can be seen is mere shadows, abstract forms projected on old walls made of concrete; no-one wants to see those monstrously unaccepted shapes; no-one wants to be looking intently at that old medieval boarding house blackened walls; no-one dares to do so: thus, people pass by, just as the clouds do in an October cloudy day; for no apparent reason. Not so far from the house, what appears to be an old man is laying down, barely covered in rugs, upon the dirty pavement. This is not the first night he has to stay outdoors, completely alone if it was not for all those drunk crowds trudging back home. But tonight he decided to lay *there*, close enough to the boarding house, for some unknown reason. People just avoid him disgusted, as if there was not another human being, deep down all that dirty face and rugs, laying there. He is taking a nap; an old bottle of red wine resting beside him; his breath going slow now, because he is dreaming: of a better life, where people *do* care about him. Every now and again one can see him smile; it is a warm night after all, and despite the sadness in his tortured life, he still smiles though only in dreams. Some sort of sweet thoughts are being rendered only for his eyes; he keeps smiling now whilst that warm wind caresses his dirty black hair smoothly: back then, there was *a wife* and *a daughter;* foggy images trying to shape themselves just for him. The alcohol makes all disappear, but not quite yet: there are still those blurred images he can summon whilst dreaming. He thinks: *That's not fair!* But still, he keeps seeing those images coming from the past, where love and happiness used to shake hands almost every day; no-one gives a damn but if they did, they would see an old sad man quivering all over, tears rolling down his cheeks, brushing some of the glued filth on his face away; *Don't leave me!,* he cries all of a sudden, lifting his left hand, reaching out; *Stay!,* he begs. Then, he awakes and opens his eyes, looking around, disoriented. Once again, he does not know where he is exactly. That's why he has to guess. *Ah,* he recalls, I *decided to have a nap over here! I was on my way to...* Where? It does not matter, not really, not now; he stands up, rubbing his eyes, putting some dirt back on his face in doing so. He intends to go find another place to sleep. He feels something is not exactly right over there. Probably the alcohol, that may be. No much luggage to pack; merely some stolen bedlinen among old newspapers and that bottle of red wine, now completely empty, but still useful for further uses. Now that he is packed, he is free to go: it is a warm night after all, and he feels like walking for a while. Behind him, not so far away, there's a dim light visible from the outside by the boarding house front door. He does not notice it because he is now leaving the other way. There it is, that light, as if someone had decided to turn it on. The old man is starting to get further, further, from the house, and now one who could be standing by the same slightly illuminated front door looking at him, wouldn't see much of that old drunk and sad man; just a small dark figure mingling with the night.

In a flash, there is no figure at all. Just the murmurs of the crowds laughing and bottles and cups clinking against each other from afar. There's no-one close enough to the boarding house now, and the place where the old man laid down looks like an immense gap; a thunder seems to scream fiercely up there, and the warm wind has decided to find a replacement in the form of a suddenly brutal and cold one blowing spuriously; sweet night no more. And there, right by the front door, the light starts flickering briefly, until there is no light at all. The entire household now remains silent and dark once again; just a sombre structure, another old medieval house no-one pays attention to; surrounded by two lovely canals, settled in a tranquil street quite far from the tourist attractions of the city.

He was standing by the front door; it was difficult to ring the door whilst carrying the city map on his left hand and grabbing hold of his huge bag with his right; travelling didn't suite him at all, but there he was; waiting for someone to come out and greet him from that old boarding house guts. At least it was cool out there; the flight from Barcelona turned out to be a burden, but surely not on purpose: the airline he flew with had had some awful delays on almost all its flights, so instead of arriving in the city by daylight, it was almost dark. Some cold wind was jerking his map violently, but he didn't care: all he wanted was to get in the house, where he would be fairly protected from that cold wind and any other dangers that unknown foreign city had in store for him. He was about to ring a second time when the front door opened. A good-looking woman in her sixties appeared, smiling:

"Welcome! You must be the guest from Barcelona!"

"I am, indeed", he said, smiling back at her.

"Let me help you with your luggage; there's a narrow staircase here."

She got out of the house in order to get his bag, and in doing so, allowed him to catch a glimpse of the boarding house interior. As she said, he could see part of a steep narrow staircase, with a white wooden rail, starting almost by the front door and leading to the other three house storeys. He came in, followed by his landlady, who was lifting his huge bag exclaiming:

"Wow, it's heavy!"

She rested the bag upon the doormat, turning her back on him briefly to shut the front door. He looked around, but he couldn't see much more than the staircase and the front door; he was standing in some sort of a corridor, with two white closed doors on his left, that very staircase on his right, and nothing else in front of him.

"If you don't mind, I'll call my husband to help me out with your bag", said she, smiling.

He nodded. It was a huge bag, very huge indeed, so he felt a bit guilty for not even trying to handle it himself. But looking carefully at that staircase, he was sure he would not be able to achieve such a thing without either harming himself or breaking something. That white wooden rail, for instance.

"Hello, welcome to our home!", said a cheerful voice on his left; he turned back to face it. A tall thin man wearing glasses passed him quickly, smiling, scratching a patch on his head. After studying the huge bag for a moment, he said: "Okay, there we go!" He grabbed the bag with his right hand and, in no time, was headed for the second floor. "It's not *that* heavy, after all." he said, "I dare say it is not as heavy as it is huge" With that, the bag was resting right in the second floor of the boarding house, and he could go upstairs now, walking behind his landlady. They ended up in another corridor, with three wooden white doors, only one of them opened. They entered the room; he could see a number painted black over the wooden door: *one*, it said.

"Well, this is it!", said his landlady. Her husband was going downstairs again, excusing himself.

"Oh, this is lovely!", he said, looking at every single detail in that bedroom. Fresh yellow dahlias greeted him with such a sweet fragrance; the bed was covered in white and clean bedlinen; he could discern a huge window behind a curtain. Upon the bed table, a lamp with a ceramic-base was scarcely illuminating the entire bedroom.

"Thank you, you are so kind. Before I leave you," said she, "breakfast's at 7:30."

He nodded. She started her way out when she seemed to remember something quite out of the blue, and turning back added:

"If you want a cup of tea, or even a coffee, you've got plenty of that in your room." Then, she pointed at a table beside the bed. Upon it rested a *nespresso* machine and a kettle, both surrounded by capsules, an obscene variety of teas and infusions, sugar lumps, silver teaspoons and lots of lots of other things he did not know of.

"Great!", he said, smiling. "I love having tea and coffee!"

"Now, I'll leave you. See you tomorrow, have a good night sleep.", she was getting out of the bedroom, so he said quickly before seeing her disappear downstairs:

"I know I will!"


3


The running water woke him up.

According to the boarding house's website, there were two guest rooms. The room where he was staying was one-numbered, so it was fairly evident to think the second one being upstairs, right on the second floor. Obviously, his landlady would explain a lot of new things to him during the breakfast, and maybe some of this new information would be related to the second room as well. After all, it was a bit naïve to think himself the only guest lodging there. Thus, he guessed the other guest was taking a shower. He had a look at his wristwatch, which was by then resting on the bed table, facing him. It was obscenely late to have a shower: 3:30 am. Bloody hell, when one was staying in a boarding house surely one was supposed to behave quite in a different way, no wonder why. But maybe that other guest upstairs was not aware of such a thing. *"Leave it by now,"* he said to himself, *"maybe it's just tonight."* That perfectly could be.

However, he was sleepy no more. He got up from the bed and went close to the table supporting that huge amount of teas and coffees. Beside the kettle, there was an *aquafina* bottle of still water. He poured some of it in the kettle, turning it on. Opposite the table was a comfortable settee; he had a seat there whilst waiting for the water to boil. Had it not been for that water running all the pipes down from the second guest room, that would have been a peaceful night, very peaceful indeed. The kettle stopped the hissing quite immediately, releasing the power button, so he knew the water was ready. He got up, putting himself in front of that magnificent assortment of teas and infusions. After pondering for a while, he came to a decision: a lovely cup of *Earl Grey* would do.

He went back to that settee, this time holding the cup of tea with his right hand. He had a few sips before closing his eyes momentarily, trying to make that annoying sound of running water disappear. He could not, so he opened his eyes again looking a bit upset. *"I told you!"*, he seemed to hear someone whispering in his ears, *"I told you not to come!"* That probably was his wife, an old but yet sweet voice, coming from the past. It was a bit late to do otherwise, so why bother? There he was, hearing voices. He smiled briefly; travelling was something he intended to do in order to stay away from his own wretched life, going further and even much much further every now and again, as if trying to escape. Curiously, that place, that boarding house, was reminding him of *her*: an old glorious image belonging to maybe the only past he would like to recall. For a moment, that smell of fresh dahlias was replaced completely with her perfume; he looked around as if searching for her; but apart from him, there was no-one in that bedroom. That intense scent remained, so he got up leaving the cup of tea upon the table where it belonged, and looked around one last time. Still nothing to see. He nodded tiredly; he was starting to fall asleep again, so it was a good idea to go back to bed. He came close to the dahlias, smelling them. Their perfume was that of hers.

*"I miss you"*, he said, his face buried in yellow dahlias, *"I miss you so much"*, he added, still inhaling that fierce fragrance from the dahlias, closing his eyes in order to smell them more intently.

Above him, some steps could be heard. The other guest was apparently getting out of the shower, and was due to bed; so that first night in that old medieval European city, the boarding house would have been in deep silence again if it had not been for some tears of insurmountable sorrow being shed in that very room, where a man was letting some fresh yellow dahlias conceal his face.

29

## 4

. "I heard the other guest having a shower," he said to his landlady quite out of the blue. They were in the dining room, beside the kitchen, in what he could understand would be the basement in any other house placed in Barcelona. He was seated at a huge wooden table, where all was delicately set: a crystal jug containing home made orange juice right in front of him; silver cutlery on his left, beside a white linen napkin; some bread and pane cakes put upon a big ceramic plate, a bit far from his reach it has to be said; a fruit salad made of water melon, apple and candied pineapple; a smoky teapot upon a silver tray to avoid the wood to be damaged; a white cup made of expensive porcelain surely in order to have tea or white-coffee – though the milk was nowhere to be seen–; and last but not least some ham on a crystal recipient, on his right.

"Oh, surely it was a dream," she said smiling, "because you are the only guest in this house right now."

He looked up, frowning: "Am I?"

"You bet", she responded, still smiling. A bell could be heard from the kitchen. "Oh!," she exclaimed, "the oven!"

She went to the kitchen, coming back after a bit carrying another plate filled with *croissants*. She put the plate upon the table, beside the teapot, moving the silver tray from where it rested slightly towards the table's centre, in order to make some additional room.

"Don't eat them right away; they are still hot." she warned him.

"Don't worry, I won't."

She went to the kitchen again and came back with a cup of tea. She took a seat on his left, by the garden's door.

"So, am I the only guest? Is that so?" he asked her again.

She sipped her tea before responding: "Well, that certainly is."

He nodded. That was a bit odd, but he was starving. Maybe that was not the right moment to think about such matters; later on, perhaps. After all, that breakfast looked really tasty. He tried that fruit salad first.

"It's good." he said, still chewing.

She put the cup upon a coaster before uttering: "You are really kind, thank you."

He looked at her for a while. She was a good-looking woman, despite the fact she was probably in her early sixties. He was really bad at guessing people's age, but still he thought her husband was surely a lucky man. He stopped surveying her briefly to let his gaze stroll quite chaotically around the dining room walls, where certain portraits hang. He, himself, did not have portraits hanging on his flat walls. He had never fancied them. Maybe, he said to himself on one such an occasion, it was because it was sad to look at them for they belonged to a far away past, like stolen moments from an ancient life due to cease; those ones hanging from his landlady's house walls reminded him of that very same dreadful feeling.

"Am I going to have tomorrow's breakfast all by myself, like this morning?" he wanted to know.

"I'm afraid there is no other guest coming." she admitted.

"Well, at least that means I'm going to be so tranquil here." he said, cheerful.

Her eyes glow fleetingly. He had finished the fruit salad and now was drinking the orange juice quite eagerly.

"It's been a while since the second room was occupied." she said almost in a whisper.

"Why's that?" he inquired, leaving the empty jug upon the table again. She sighed, arms-folded, lifting her head a bit. He helped himself with the teapot. "What's in there?" he asked.

"Strong coffee."

"Great!" he said, pouring some of it in that porcelain cup. It was black, indeed. "So, tell me, is anything the matter with that second room?"

"As far as I know, nothing that cannot be mended." she stated.

"I see, so what is it then?"

She sighed again, staring at him.

"You don't want to hear a story like this one in your first day here." she observed.

"I'd love to."

She smiled. Indeed; such a good-looking woman, nonetheless. She looked a bit nervous though; probably because of the tale she was about to tell him; or maybe because he was a total stranger in that house, not to mention the fact he was from abroad, and despite so she intended to relate that tale to him. She unfolded her arms and sat up in the chair.

"Okay, I think this story deserves to be told, after all." she said.

"I'm all ears."

She got up and started to go around the dinning table. Finally, she decided to stay by the garden's door. Turning her back on him, she opened it; some sun rays penetrated through the room making the silver tray glow.

"You see, today's really warm", she said. "But this house's always cold."

"I'm not cold." he admitted, trying to sound polite.

31

"Of course you are not, I put the central heating on early this morning." She turned around.

"That may be, then." he admitted, dryly.

"Anyway," she went on, "there are days when even turning the central heating on it's not enough."

"Is that so?"

She did not respond. He looked at the garden for a bit; it was cosy. A picnic table laid in the middle, with some wooden benches around it. A huge plant pot could be seen on its right, its base made of porcelain and depicting some sort of an angel with unfolded wings, crying.

"We've been here for five years, you know," she said, "only five years."

"I see."

"During all this time, this residence has been a peaceful place to be, as a guest, for professors and tourists equally."

She stopped talking and looked at her wristwatch. Then, as if remembering something, she asked him: "Aren't you late or something?"

"Oh, no, not at all. I've got plenty of time. Please, do continue."

She nodded, concealing her wristwatch under a sleeve. "This house was not a boarding house at all at first, did you know that?" it was a rhetoric question, so he decided not to interrupt her, "So, we bought it five years ago to start this enterprise, you see. Many guests have come to enjoy a short stay among these very walls, most of them have come back twice or even more times." She stopped talking and added: "Oh, sorry, I did not mean to boast."

"You didn't." he assured her.

"You are extremely kind," she said. For the best part of a minute, she said nothing. He was sure she was trying to find the right words to go on, the best way to explain such a tale without making a fool of herself or something of that sort. Eventually, she continued: "Well, one day an old gentleman knocked at our door. He was a writer in need of some peaceful place to write. Our second room was available by then, so we took him in." She got up, getting her empty cup of tea. Then, excusing herself, she went to the kitchen where she poured some more tea in it. From there, she went on: "He was polite and clean, and he stayed for one whole month. The weird thing is that he had breakfast in there, you know," he could see her in the kitchen pointing with her index finger at the ceiling, "and he never came downstairs to have breakfast in here."

"You are quite right there, that's a bit odd."

"Oh, we have had some guests quite fond of their own loneliness, but even those ones wanted to have breakfast in the dining room, though at a really odd times." she smiled. "Anyway, he had breakfast every single day in his room. I put his breakfast upon a silver tray and every morning, at 6:00am, I was due to bring it upstairs."

"Quite an annoying thing to do, I guess." he observed.

"I was exhausted because in order to serve him the breakfast, I had to prepare it at least half an hour before. That meant I woke up every morning at about 5:15am."

She came back from the kitchen, still holding her cup of tea. She was yet to have a sip.

"So, what happened?" he asked.

"One cold and bleak morning, I brought his breakfast upstairs, as usual. I knocked at his door, but I got no answer. Therefore, I thought him asleep, so I left the silver tray upon a chair by his door and went downstairs again."

As if trying to recreate that very moment, she rested her cup of tea upon the wooden dinning table. She looked a bit pale.

"Are you feeling all right?"

"Oh, yes, don't worry about me."

She sipped some tea from her cup. It seemed that that lovely cup of tea was calming her. That odd tale was starting to get extremely interesting, but he could almost foresee where she was getting at.

"So, what did you do?" he asked.

"Not much, really. I did my housework; I went to the supermarket for some supplies, then I came back home in order to clean the first room up. I did not think to go upstairs to check on him. I was just fairly busy with my own stuff."

"I see."

"So, the next morning I realized I had forgotten to get the silver tray back, you know."

He stared at her intently. She had another sip of tea.

"Thus, I went upstairs to get it back." she went on. "You can imagine how I felt as soon as I saw the silver tray untouched, still laying right upon that chair."

She paused briefly; he took advantage of it and poured some more strong coffee in his porcelain cup. He didn't want to miss a word of her story. She remained silent all this process along, looking at the ceiling.

"So, what happened next?" he asked her.

"I tried to talk to him through the closed door. I said: *Weren't you hungry*? But I got no answer. I couldn't hear any sound in there."

"Didn't you open the door?"

She smiled. "Not immediately; we've got some principles involved when it comes to our guests' privacy, you know." she said with a serious look on her face. "I resolved to call on my husband, who were on some errands at that moment."

She took a deep breath and got up again, quite unexpectedly. She was in evident disgrace, she was not comfortable talking about that matter and still, she had been the one bringing that very same matter up. To some extend, she reminded him of his wife. Those old days before the illness set foot in their home had been the best of their lives. He found himself every now and again thinking about her, even now, amidst that foreign city, whilst listening to that spooky tale of unknown guests entering their rooms and not getting out of them for days on end. That fragrance he could smell at night, somehow replacing that other one belonging naturally to those fresh yellow dahlias, and the feeling she was actually in there, beside him, though invisible, depressed him. Not a single spoken word coming from that landlady would make him think of better days now: that seemed foolish; her words were darkening his days instead.

"He came quite quickly," she started again, "grabbed the bedroom's key just in case and opened the door. It wasn't locked."

He left the cup upon the table, before the plate where some rest of fruit salad could be seen. Then, entangling his hands, said:

"What did you see in there?"

She sighed. He could feel some dreadfulness surrounding them right there, in that dining room. Before knowing anything about that weird scary tale, it looked like charming and homely. Unluckily, it was charming and homely no more.

She sat on that chair on his left again, for the last time that morning, and with evident discomfort, she managed to utter some words due to conclude that tale:

"He was dead. Dead as a doornail."

5

*There's no such things as ghosts*, he recalled her saying. His wife was laying on the marital bed, hardly noticing he was right there, because the illness had took her eyes as well. The bedroom was surrounded by fresh flowers: red roses and red tulips. He stood beside her, resting his back against the window frame, observing her sink. The doctors had told him already she was not supposed to last much longer. According to their medical opinion, it was a miracle that she was still alive. *"Oh,"* he said to her, *"but you are wrong there. They do exist."* She moved her head slightly, as if trying to accommodate herself in such a way that, if anything, she could keep the false illusion of being able to actually *see* him. He looked at her, and in doing so, he watered his eyes. She looked so fragile, so weak, so dependable, that he could barely stand it. *"It is you, who is wrong."* she assured him, smiling. She could still smile, despite all the pain, and he dried his eyes and reached her bed. He knelt down beside her. He caressed her forehead, feeling the coldness on her skin, which was white as bone. After so many years, *this*. He tried to cheer up; he did not want to show sadness in front of her; he wanted to be strong: she deserved that very much. But that sight was insurmountable: she was dying right there, on that very same bed where they had had sex so many and glorious times, and now she was almost like an empty vessel, and he was trembling all over, and he wanted to let her know they *did* exist, the ghosts, they *did really* exist, they *had to*, otherwise that would mean he would be absolutely alone without the smallest chance of meeting her one last time, in that so far *hereafter*, where tearful souls would be reunited for ages on end.

It was all in vain; she passed away that same night. It was quite a shock. He did not want to see anyone; he stayed at home for a whole month barely feeding himself. When he decided it was about time to get out of the house, he was all skin and bones. The moment he set foot on the street, he felt sick and vomited. He started wandering around the streets, trying to pull himself together. *Life is quite a different thing to cope with now*, he thought. *That last smile is there all the time; a grin on a dead face; long black hair rotting itself, spread all over the marital bed; from it dark and dirty threads emerge, looking nasty and dreadful; and her white face is now surrounded by them, and he does not intend to brush them aside; he knows they are dead but somehow alive as well, and they look like daring him to do so, so that he can end up trapped in them. No way, he says to himself, I am going to touch them; so he does not. It is dark in there and he is cold, and he wonders if that's because of her. I love you, he says to her though he does know she is gone already, and there is no way she can hear his uttered words now, because what is laying there, right now, it's just a carcass.*

This time it was the phone that woke him up. It was not late; he had been dozing for maybe half an hour on that comfortable settee. That could explain why, at first, it was so difficult for him to reach out for the cell phone, resting all by itself upon the bedroom's carpeted floor.

"Yes?"

"How are things going, pal?" asked a voice on the other side of the line. He stood up, a bit surprised. Pacing the bedroom up and down, he held the cell phone tight against his right ear.

"Doctor!" he exclaimed.

"Yeah, *that* is me!"

After his wife's death, a lot of things had changed for the worse. Therefore, certain help was required. That doctor speaking now on the phone was the first form *that* help had adopted; a cheerful psychiatrist expert on amending people's life using an astonishing assortment of legal drugs. It was his idea, in fact, to get out of that house and go on travelling; *no drugs this time*, he would say smiling, *there is no need to do so, not yet.* So, after much more pondering, he decided he would go to Holland.

"Oh, you know, not so brilliant" he admitted, resignedly.

The Doctor came to a silence for a long while. He waited for him to continue, and in realizing he did not, he added:

"It is not your fault."

That appeared to work, for the Doctor hurried to say:

"Oh, I see, it is okay. Maybe I could prescribe you some drugs, after all."

"Not at all, I'll be fine."

He could hear the doctor sighting on the other side of the line. He could even imagine him seated on that black-furred armchair; upon the desk a laptop running the screen-saver; some papers spread out all upon the wooden desk in such an obsessive and ordered manner; a pile of sorted folders standing on its left side, a bit far from reach, with big blue printed out letters: surely on top of that same pile there would be the one summarizing his own life.

"Is anything the matter?" the doctor asked him, doubtful.

He took his time before answering:

"Doctor, do you believe in ghosts?"

"What sort of question is *that*?"

He smiled. *Ghosts*; no way he was thinking seriously about having a ghost right upstairs. However, that first night had proved relatively plausible.

"Oh, I've been having, you know, *experiences*."

"It is not *that*; it's just you are a bit down in the mouth. That's all." observed the doctor.

"That perfectly may be, but still ..."

"You are talking nonsense. There is no such things as ghosts."

"So my wife said."

But he was not so sure now. According to his landlady, someone had died upstairs, and now the second room was empty. Despite so, he could hear the water running and the steps of someone above getting out of the shower and going to bed. That was not pure imagination, that was something real. He could possibly need some drugs to get on, but that did not change the *matter-of-fact* situation he got right there, in that old Dutch medieval boarding house.

"You see? Put your mind at rest; go on a tourist rampage or something!" the doctor suggested.

"I intend to pay the tower of the city a visit late this afternoon." he said mechanically.

"That sounds great!"

"They say it has forty hundred and sixty five steps to get to its very top."

The doctor talked again. He could catch a slight change on his voice: maybe now, turning the conversation to that area of climbing towers and sight-seeing the city, was something he really wanted to hear. He was a psychiatrist, after all.

"Enjoy the climbing, then! Keep me posted, okay?"

"I will; thanks for calling, Doctor."

"My pleasure."

The doctor was the first one to hang up the phone. He left his cell phone upon the bed, looking out the window behind the curtain. It was getting dark again, maybe time to go downstairs and fix some dinner. His landlady told him so: he was free to go to the kitchen any time to prepare his own food. However, he was not hungry. He put the TV on. A sheet showing an exhaustive TV-channel list laid upon the bed table. He studied it largely, and finally he came to a decision and put the BBC World Service on, making himself comfortable upon the bed. Some awful problem related to Spanish cucumbers was the main European authorities' concern, and according to the news, some German people had died of e.coli already, as a direct consequence of eating those very same Spanish cucumbers. He was astonished, but not as astonished as he had been after knowing there was *no-one* upstairs.

*"I miss you"*, he said. His voice sounded sad and hopeless in that almost quiet bedroom, because he kept the TV volume at a minimum; he did not want to annoy his landlady and her husband. He looked at the place where those yellow dahlias had stood; they were gone. In their place, looking majestic, rested some big and beautiful red tulips. *Of course*, he thought, *this is Holland after all. So why not? Some red tulips, sure*. Maybe it was the tulips' fragrance, or maybe it was because he was tired, or maybe it was even because the British voices coming from the TV were flawless and, being so, were, in fact, almost mesmerising him; but the fact is: he fell asleep, and he dreamed of her, and he cried although he did not notice it because he was dreaming; and his tears went all his face down until pooling upon the bed, where small stains appeared almost immediately. He quivered all over briefly, as if the dream was hard to cope with; after a while he was at ease, breathing regularly, eyes-closed and arms-crossed upon his pit; he was crying no more, so the stains upon the bedlinen dried and vanished; the TV was merely a rumour and the night had finally fell down; his landlady and her husband were sleeping peacefully one storey below; there was no-one to be seen strolling the streets, and the canals reflected the moonlight recklessly; from time to time some distant voices could be heard because there were some tourists coming back to their hotels and boarding houses; but not there, in that peaceful street, fairly far from the bustle of

that ancient city; so, neither his landlady nor her husband heard the door's latch moving; neither did he. Otherwise, they would have got up in order to go quickly to see who *that* was; for no-one apart from the guest staying in the first room was supposed to be there or to have the key to get in; and most likely, in doing so, they would have seen something they had not managed to comprehend, not with the use of their left-side of the Sperry's model for the human brain; for although it was a fact that the door got open, no-one was standing there to be seen, and despite so the door was widely opened, as if someone big – or maybe we could possibly say fat – was having some sort of difficulties to get through; and what about observing the door, after a couple of seconds, shut itself again slowly, and then hear the key acting on the lock? Surely we could continue our odd description in telling that *that* was not just the only supernatural event for that night, because right then the narrow staircase seemed to complain itself by emitting some creaking noises, the usual ones one could hear when someone was going upstairs, aiding himself with that wooden white rail; but that would not be over until hearing the second room's door open and close itself again, followed by some small pressure faintly perceptible through the ceiling, in case one had stood one storey right below.

6

"Did you sleep well?"

That was his landlady in her way from the kitchen, holding a silver tray with a white plate full of home-made ham upon it. She put the tray on the dinning table and smiled at him.

"Oh yes, I did." he responded.

She nodded and took a seat opposite him.

"So, no odd noises in the middle of the night this time, right?"

"Nope."

"It looks like there is no ghost, after all, does it not?"

"I suppose it does, yes." he said, sipping some coffee.

She nodded once again, letting her back rest against the wooden chair. Her look was somehow different that morning; he could barely fathom why. She looked older, as if she had been awake all night long.

"Are you okay?" he asked her.

She took her time to answer:

"No, not really."

He put his cup of coffee, now almost empty, upon its saucer. Staring at her, he folded his arms and frowned: "So?"

"This morning I found the second room's door locked." she said without hesitation.

"Is that so terrible?"

"I did not lock the door; neither did my husband."

"I see."

"It is common to give a pair of keys to our guests, as you do know, to allow them to lock their bedrooms for security reasons and to get in and out whenever they please; there is no curfew in this house, as you well know. Most of them don't lock their doors, because they don't feel like doing so in this very house, and that's something of the utmost importance to us." She paused briefly, sighting. Then, she continued: "But that other guest I told you yesterday morning about, *that*, that was really a paranoid one."

"Was he?"

"Oh, yes, he truly was." she said, disgusted.

"So he usually locked his bedroom's door every time he was out, is that so?"

"Pretty much."

He nodded and added, smiling sadly: "My wife would've done the same."

"But it could possibly be I was wrong, you know, and maybe it was *me* who locked that door. I'm getting on a bit, and I've got memory lacks from time to time." she admitted, regretfully. "The problem is", she went on, "I looked for those keys; not the ones we keep for ourselves, but the ones I normally give to any guest staying in that room."

She stopped talking, as if trying to find the right words to describe what was in her mind. That was a dull morning; the dining room was barely illuminated by all the lamps hanging from the ceiling, and even the opened garden's door seemed to project weird shadows on the dining room's walls, thus hardening the darkness inside. That house, the one which looked so lovely and homely, now, little by little, was becoming something quite the contrary: a place where shadows were painting walls black; a place where not even the central heating was able to produce the slightest warmth; a place where too many memories melted down like ice, composing a bleak atmosphere of sad and gloomy remembrances no-one could possibly bear.

"I could not find them." she concluded, looking down as if she was ashamed of herself.

"Did you use the other keys, the ones you've got, to get in the room?" he questioned.

"Yes, I did."

"So? Did you see something in there? Anything?"

She looked at him vividly and nodded widely. Taking a deep breath, she said:

39

"The shower."

"The shower? What was wrong with it?"

"I clean the shower myself at least twice per week; more often if a guest leaves and there is another one coming to the same room." she explained tiredly. "So, it was supposed to remain that way."

"You mean..."

"I mean what I did see when I got in that room: the shower was not clean any more, as if someone had used it. It could have been used that first night of your arrival, when you thought you heard the water running."

"You are kidding me!" he shouted, astonished.

"I fear I am not."

Upon the wooden dinning table, more or less in its centre, a sole honey wax candle rested quite unaware of a cold wind entering the dining room through the garden's opened door, all of a sudden. He stared at it for a while, observing how that wind was blowing the candle slightly and not on purpose, until she got up and shut the door almost violently; then, the candle was still offering its honeyed light and fragrance, but just briefly, because after not so long its flame was finally extinguished.

"According to your own words then," he stated, "there *is* a ghost in this very house, and it *does* have those keys."

She went to the kitchen and came back after a minute holding a match box. She intended to light the candle again, but oddly she did not manage to do so. She gave up, eventually.

"I know it sounds a bit crazy, but it does look that way." she confessed, putting the match box upon the table, beside the honey wax candle.

For the best part of a minute, neither of them said anything. Too many things to ponder; too many weird events to consider.

Finally, it was him who said:

"I think we should find out more about that guest you told me."


7


It came to happen he got a friend who had never spent a sole night away from home. Odd, certainly, because that very same friend of his was, at that time, about forty years old. He tried to convince him to do the other way round, that is, to get away from home for, let's say, a whole year.

*To taste it*, as he put it once. The idea was to show him good things could happen when one was out there, in an unknown environment. That was before she passed away, so he himself was not willing to be far from home for such a long time, obviously, but still he could suggest so to his friend. When she died, it was the Doctor who suggested him just the same.

"Catch a plane; go see the world out there", the Doctor would say to him one rainy morning.

Being alone was hard to cope with. Sometimes, whilst wondering around the city, he saw people having beers in pubs. He wondered if he could have a seat, alone, amidst that very same people and ask the waiter for a beer. Would that beer taste the same as the ones they were drinking? He feared it would not. So, instead of taking a seat over there, he just passed by, going back home. He could remember perfectly well how he met his wife. He was not that sort of handsome man well known among the women; on the contrary, he was pretty ugly: almost bald, with a big nose; as long as he was sweating gross trails of acne were clearly visible upon his skin. Besides, he did not socialize much, there it laid the difficulty of meeting women. So, it was quite a surprise how they bumped into each other that Saturday evening. He was a bit crossed that evening because some sort of an unsolved problem at work, so instead of staying at home as usual, he went for a drink. He walked into a bar not so far away from home, merely a matter of pragmatism: in case he got ill-drunk, he could reach home more or less safely. The bar was dark and stank of smoke and fries; but he did not pay attention to that: he got in, had a seat at a table placed in a far corner, and waited for the waiter to come. Instead of a waiter, it turned out it was a waitress, and quite beautiful. After so many beers, but right before he started to feel awfully drowsy, she asked him if he was all right. He responded he was not, that was why he was having lots of lots of pure cheap beer: to brush all his problems away. She said *that* was wrong; life was, essentially, marvellous and he was mistaken in throwing it away like that; he looked up and smiled, but just briefly; it was then when their eyes seemed to meet for the first time that night. She was holding another bottle of cold beer upon a tray, but instead of putting it on the table, she turned around and disappeared among all that smoke and dim light. He could make out some words she uttered right before vanishing in thin air:

"You had enough."

He stayed there for a while, despite the fact he had beer no more. The bar's interior looked fairly gloomy but that was the kind of atmosphere he was looking for; thus, he decided to stay seated at that empty table, letting time pass by. Half an hour later, she returned carrying a white plate; she put it upon the table, right in front of him. On it, he could see a tasty sandwich made of ham.

"Eat it." she said.

"I'm not hungry." he admitted, folding his arms.

41

She smiled at him: "You must be, it is just you didn't realize yet."

After saying so, she took a seat beside him. He could smell her perfume and her proximity, somehow, scared him. So he tried to say, politely, that he was not hungry at all, so she'd better be going to attend to other customers, thank you very much. She did not respond, looking at him a bit amused.

"Whatever it is, it cannot be *that* bad." she said, almost in a whisper.

"How could you possibly know that?" he inquired.

She sighed.

"I've been through a nightmare lately."

"Have you?"

"Indeed."

He toyed with the plate for a while, not feeling hungry yet but almost. She went on:

"I was married to an English man for ten years, and I worked in the United Kingdom for almost seven out of those very ten years. I lived in a small town, a stone town as they called it: *Stamford*."

He nodded.

"I see, and now you are back, is that so?"

She smiled bitterly.

"I wouldn't say that, but well, all things considered, maybe it *is* so."

He looked a bit confused, so he asked her: "Where's the nightmare in that?"

"At first, I was quite enjoying my new life there, but after one whole year I got bored." she elaborated. Her eyes expressed sadness. "So I guess I could say I've being bored for almost six entire years."

"What about your husband? Are you still married?"

"Not at all. I got a divorce." said she, triumphantly. "Now, I don't feel like going abroad any more. I want to stay here, in my home country, until the day I die."

He started to feel a bit hungry. He stopped toying with the plate and grabbed the sandwich quickly, startling her.

"It turns out I am a bit hungry." he confessed, biting it.

"I knew it."

He ate the sandwich without uttering a word; she stared at him all the time. As soon as he finished the whole thing, she smiled and said:

"Aren't you going to tell me what the matter is?"

He shrugged.

"I don't know. Should I?"

He pondered for a while. It was starting to get late, so he had to think about going to work the next morning. He was a bit drunk, though not as drunk as he would have been in case she had served him beers all evening long, which was the very first idea, it had to be said. Thus, instead of pouring down his misery, he got up and in no time was headed home, leaving her in that bar, seated at that table, where an empty plate rested all by itself  quite near to the edge; he did not come back that evening; not even the next one: it took almost an entire week until he dared to do so. She was still there, of course, because she worked there, so they met again and they had a little chat about trivial matters. This time, he did not drink beer; he contented himself by having coffee and talking openly to her. It was a relief to realize that, after so many years, he finally had found someone to talk to; from then on he walked into that bar every time and again, and all those visits converged in an actual date: they went to the cinema to watch a British film titled *Never Let Me Go*, based on the novel written by *Kazuo Ishiguro;* it was near its ending when a certain Miss Geraldine would say: *"We didn't have the gallery to see into your souls; we had the gallery to see if you had souls at all."* At those words, spoken so coldly, he could not help it but water his eyes; she realized that and put her left hand over his right one gently. He turned his head slightly towards her in order to look at her face. A sole tear seemed to be trapped in its way down her cheek; he made it disappear by touching it smoothly with one of his fingers; she closed her eyes almost instinctively and he wondered if his touch would be cold; her skin was warm so he did not  command his finger to get away immediately: he allowed his finger to rest right there upon her skin for a bit longer instead, thinking all along if he would dare to move it far beyond her cheek, maybe all the way down her beautiful and unprotected neck. *"There are no deferrals,"* said another voice coming from the film, *"and there never have been."* She opened her eyes and stared at him. The film was building up to its very ending, but that did not seem to be of any importance to them; so whilst in it Madame bid her farewell to that couple of hopeless clones by saying: *"Poor creatures, I wish I could help you",* they kept staring at one another, not daring to make the slightest move, neither of them, until she put her head to rest against his shoulder whilst reaching out for his hand. *"Stop the car; I have to get out."* said a certain Tommy in the film. That scream they were not prepared to cope with; so while that Tommy was totally devastated, kneeling down upon that wet soil of England, they were quite in bad spirits: the ending came not so long after that intense bit; that very last sentence was actually a bitter statement: *"If the lives of all those who we are supposed to save are so different from the ones we live, we are all completed."*

"I think I love you." she said, still resting her head against his shoulder.

He smiled and kissed her on her forehead. *Someone finally does*, he thought.

According to his landlady, that guest got published once: *Walls* was his first and last novel's title. A young lady who lived all by herself went nuts after her father's death. Trapped in a small flat, she would spend her days knocking walls down whilst her terrified neighbours wandered when the entire building would collapse. That would happen eventually, of course, and all of them would perish irremediably, whilst she would become the sole survivor of the tragedy. *Cheerful,* he thought. Curiously, his landlady had that book somewhere in the boarding house, because when she knew who that guest was, she decided to go buy his book.

It was a heart attack. Apart from the police and a doctor, some relatives would come to the house in order to take care of his belongings, above all his laptop, where it was supposed he would have some pages from his new work; an unfinished book, probably. His death was briefly covered by a local newspaper, and she could read some vague remark on a widespread one whose name she could barely recall. She decided no guest would stay in that room, because now it was stained with angst and sorrow; her husband could not agree more with her; therefore that room would remain closed forever. About his last novel, she did not hear a word: he was extremely careful all the time so that she rarely found his laptop switched on without him being around and, besides, she had to admit she did not give a shit: the reading of *Walls* turned out to be a bit boring. When she opened that door and found him laying down upon the bed, her first thought was he was somehow sedated. It would not be after calling his name twice that she would dare to have a closer look: to her panic, he was not breathing. He was laying down face up, eyes opened, arms resting upon the white sheets; the room's guest keys glowed from his cupped left hand. On the bed table, right beside the bed lamp, a paperback edition of a book written by *Ian McEwan, Atonement,* with a bookmark slipped between pages 76 and 77, rested quite unaware of its owner's death. Apparently, he found something of the utmost importance in the last sentence in page 77, for he underlined it using a highlighter: *She would simply wait on the bridge, calm and obstinate, until events, real events, not her own fantasies, rose to her challenge, and dispelled her insignificance*. The laptop was nowhere to be seen, so she would wonder for a while where it was found in the end, and who made the discovery. Opposite the bed, standing upon a narrow marble table and in a quite impressive old vase decorated with dragons and mountains, some yellow dahlias – her preferred ones -, were withering. She hasted to get them out of that room, because it was pretty obvious to her that some odd malevolence had impregnated them, and she did not want them to die: so he put the dahlias downstairs, in her private rooms, and made some phone calls. She put them on the window-sill, hoping that some morning sun rays, slightly intensified by the filter-effect in going through the window-pane, would make them recover. Not too long after that, the boarding house would be full of strangers and she would wait outside the room, upstairs, leaning her back against the white wooden rail, worrying about her dahlias. A lot of questions would come, obviously, but there would be no further inquiries, for it was pretty evident, according to the doctor, that that guest had died of a heart attack.

When she went downstairs and she was sure there was no-one else in the house apart from her husband, she decided to check on her yellow dying dahlias. She hoped they would be better: after all she got them out of that room where only death seemed to dwell. But when she got in her private rooms, she could see that the vase was now completely empty. She heard a noise behind her, so she turned around to face it. It was her husband carrying a big blue scum bag; from there, some sterns could be seen emerging awkwardly, as if they were not just dahlias, but something else willing to escape. *What have you done?*, she asked him fiercely. He could barely respond; he looked at her instead still holding that blue scum bag full of withered dahlias, hesitated, moved his head down clumsily after a while, stared at that scum bag of his as if mystified by some ancient secret, and after his first and only unsuccessful try of making up an excuse, he was headed out of the room, stumbling whilst crossing the door, right under its frame, therefore losing his balance and making the scum bag fell upon the floor. She looked down horrified at those dying dahlias, some of them now spread upon the tiled floor, for that fall had tossed them out of the bag. *What have you done, for God's sake?*, she asked him once again, almost crying. But it was pointless; he would not be able to say a word, kneeling down upon the floor, trying to gather himself; she would not make a try to help him up, thus conveying him to a certain isolation he probably did not deserve at all, and so he would feel alone and lonely, and in his pain he would summon the same angst and sorrow that would dwell for years on end in that guests' room, only one storey above, and in doing so it would be more than just a wooden white door what they would decide to close forever. She would eventually get out of the room leaving those dahlias lying upon the tiled floor, squeezing up whilst getting past the door so that she could avoid touching her husband, who would cleverly resolve to stand still until she was nowhere to be seen.

9

"We have to trap him." he said.

From his left, seated at the dining room's table, it came her nod. "But how?" she demanded

45

to know.

He sighed and closed his eyes as if hesitating, folding his arms. It was a nice morning though a bit cold. Because he had not got out of the house yet he could not know whether the cold had, in fact, something to do with that supernatural presence upstairs or, on the contrary, a fairly plausible explanation could apply there in the form of lower temperatures; that was Holland, after all, and cold and windy days were more than common. She had put the central heating on that morning, and it seemed to him she was doing so every morning, in a desperate intent on warming the entire house up.

Finally, he opened his eyes and responded:

"Well, that ghost seems incapable of getting a door open without using a key, does it not?" he smiled briefly. He waited for her to nod once again, then went on: "So, we had to lock him up." he added, confident.

"You mean, in the room upstairs?"

"Indeed. It appears to me that's the easiest way possible, don't you think?"

She nodded for the third time that morning. Trapping a ghost was supposed to be something almost impossible, some sort of difficult task only actual experts could attempt; despite so she thought that *scheme* as foolish as it was feasible: *to trap that ghost in its own room*. Brilliant.

"And then, what?" she asked him.

"Still pondering that." he confessed.

"Well, the first idea was to keep that door closed forever, so I think it does not really matter if we have a ghost trapped in there."

She stood up and went to the kitchen to make some more strong filtered coffee. He waited for their chat to resume toying with his empty porcelain cup. That morning the adjacent garden's door was shut. A huge old golden lamp hang from the ceiling not half a meter above his head, framing him in a small circle of light. Beyond that table, the kitchen was in almost complete darkness. He turned his head to the right, in order to catch a glimpse of her working in the kitchen. He came to think about the weirdness of it all: how delicate it seemed to be that circle of light where he was enclosed in; how it was closing in, little by little, despite it was not so early in the morning and the lamp had the same number of light bulbs on; would that mean the ghost was back? He shook his head thus ostracising that idea almost immediately; he could not allow poisonous thoughts commanding his actions. He looked up at that impressive golden lamp and saw it move slightly. She came back from the kitchen carrying another silver coffee pot: she held it by its handle using her right hand, which was covered in rugs to avoid it from getting harm. In no time she was in the light circle, smiling at him dryly. She took a seat sighting, and then put the coffee pot where the empty one had stood.

"How are we going to lock him up?" she questioned.

He helped himself with the coffee, and after having a couple of sips he said:

"First, we have to watch his movements."

"It *is* a ghost, we cannot actually see him."

"We don't know that, and besides I did *not* mean to watch *him*: I meant to watch *his movements*."

"Like doors opening on their own and the staircase emitting odd noises late at night?"

"Sort of."

She nodded in silence. He looked up once again in order to check on that golden lamp. It was not moving now, not even slightly. Its stillness made him remember, though only briefly, about an old acquaintance of his whose first abroad trip had been to Liverpool; there he would buy a calendar for a present, one of those full of spectacular pictures of the city and its surroundings; that present was supposed to be for some woman or another he had never heard of; however, on one such a sad occasion, he happened to be having a beer in his acquaintance's flat – difficult to recall why -, and in his way to have a little po he saw that very same calendar still wrapped in that kind of transparent foil, resting upon a rotten wooden table, circled by rusty screws and nuts, some hammers and an old screwdriver no-one would use any more. That storeroom was full of long-time-ago forgotten things. He could not help it but get in that room and had a look at the calendar. It was completely useless. He wondered if that friend of his would be from the past, in that case maybe the calendar sill could be of some assistance. S*pace for daily appointments*, it said. He felt a bit depressed. It was a present due to cease its own frugal existence; just one year, or maybe a bit more in case its owner forgot about it some time past December; but that one was not only damned from the very beginning of its conception: it was even worse: no-one had used it, no-one had gazed at its gorgeous pictures, no-one had even unwrapped it: there it was, standing upon an old wooden table where only ineffectual tools laid, as if it was something to be ashamed of: *an error.*

"The room's door can be locked from the outside and, if you are in there and you don't have the key, you get trapped. Is that so?" he asked her.

She looked a bit embarrassed for a while.

"Yes." that was all she said.

"So that's it, then" he murmured, "we have to steal the keys from him and lock the door from the outside."

She stared at him astonished.

"How are we supposed to achieve something like that?"

47

For the best part of a minute he said nothing. He was still thinking about that run out calendar: on its back he saw twelve different pictures of Liverpool, one for each year's month: *The Albert Dock, The Metropolitan Cathedral, The Anglican Cathedral,* and among them and closer to the months belonging to the spring season *Sutton Park,* and an impressive ferry crossing the *Mersey River* by moonlight – though he had never heard of a *Mersey Ferry* crossing the river at night at all -. Despite its proximity to the river, *The Albert Dock* stood for January. When he left, his acquaintance kept drinking brutally. One month after he would be told about him being suicidal, and not long after that  he would heard about his death. He had killed himself slitting his veins, surely a painful way to die. He wondered about that calendar, had he committed suicide staring at it, still wrapped in that transparent foil and crying? He could see more or less clearly how his tears would ran all his face down until reaching the calendar, which would be probably resting upon his lap in order to gaze at it whilst his wide open wrists gushed a lot of blood off its transparent foil: oddly, he would be long dead but the calendar, under its protective cover, would be completely all right despite all the blood.

"We have to wait until he fall asleep." he responded without looking at her.

"In case we can see him."

"As I said, we don't know if he's invisible. Maybe he is, but maybe we can hear him breathing."

"Do you think he is out now?"

He looked at her finally, forcing a smile.

"I couldn't tell." he answered dryly.

He thought about his doctor, that good light-hearted psychiatrist, convincing him to explore the world; the best way of avoiding sad remembrances and cheer up. *Bloody hell,* he said to himself, *it's been just the contrary.* First it was his wife; now that old acquaintance of his and his dreadful suicide; he wondered how painful would be to slit one's veins, and how long would take to die that way. He resolved his acquaintance had had plenty of time to look at that bloody calendar whilst dying. He knew for sure sadness could shape one's life in such a terrible way that most people out there would choose death to live; in that context it was not a paradox: it was a *cure*.

"We have to wait for him to arrive in his room, I'm afraid." he said after a while.

"Hidden?"

"Exactly." he sipped some filtered coffee and smiled at her, "Maybe under his bed."

"But first we should be sure he's out, don't you think?"

He nodded.

"How?" she asked staring at him.

"We can go to his room now, and check if its door's locked."

"I did not lock the door when I found out about the shower and the keys," she admitted. "so it shouldn't be."

"If he's in there." he added, gloomily.

"Last time that door was locked, it was early in the morning." she reminded him.

"You're right." he said looking at his wristwatch. "If he's out, that door should be locked; we will wait otherwise."

"What about the window? Do you think he could ..." she started.

"No way," he cut in on her suddenly, "he's still using keys for God's sake!"

She remained silent, giving his thoughts another opportunity to drift around.

*There's no such things as ghosts,* his wife said once. Now, he had to deal with an odd one, one incapable of getting doors open without a key; one having showers irritably late at night; one being as paranoid as when it was alive; what sort of ghost could that possibly be? He had to admit it: that entire situation was far beyond anything else he could ever think of. What was it what he wanted? He had another sip of strong coffee and sighed. She helped herself with some tea; that morning the fresh fruit salad was still resting on his white plate, untouched. He was not hungry. He had had the orange juice and some ham, and that would be all for that day. So, what was the plan? Get into his room: either he would be out or he would be right there. In case the door was locked, it was more than probable he would be out. She told him so: he was a paranoid. All the time he had locked his door during the time he had spent outdoors. And, apparently, even now, he was still acting the same way. So the idea was simple: to wait for him under the bed, not making the slightest noise, and hope for the best: he was that sort of weird ghost having showers and getting doors open using a mere key, that he probably would have to take a nap. That most certainly was, he thought without any doubts. He was sure the ghost would be somehow a physical presence, though maybe invisible; anyway, he thought it would be feasible to lay down upon the carpeted floor, right under the bed, and still hear or even see some pressure upon it at the precise instant the ghost would decide to go to bed. Then they would wait until it was safe to steal the keys – which, he guessed, would be dangling from the door's keyhole -.

"Who will be? I mean, the one waiting in the room." she asked him.

"Me." he sounded as if he had made up his mind entirely.

"I see." she looked at him sadly and after a moment's hesitation, she said: "It can't be any dangerous, can it?"

He did not respond.

"Damn!" she exclaimed.

He wanted that ghost trapped, stuck in that room upstairs. *It is you who is wrong*, his wife said that last night, laying in her death's bed, blind. Remembrances were driving him crazy; he pitied his doctor, because now that trip to Holland had proved itself absolutely useless: instead of keeping him away from suicidal and dark thoughts, there he was: dealing with old dreadful and sad memories; thinking about death almost every now and again, and wishing to capture a ghost; an actual ghost whose limited powers were forcing him to use something as earthly as that key-pair to get doors open. So he thought about his wife all along, and if a ghost could interact with the real world, then it was for granted that that very same ghost would be able to pass messages to others of the same condition, namely dead. He could remember her forehead's coldness when he touched it that last time, and how she couldn't see him though he was almost upon her and despite her illness she smelled of fresh roses. His first night in the boarding house he sensed something, something lurking in his room, willing to show up but eventually vanishing; could that be *her*? He closed his eyes and summoned her face; who cared when that ghost decided to appear? Who the hell cared why he decided to stay in that room instead of lodging elsewhere? Who cared about anything else than *a possibility*? *A connection,* he thought. That was it. The *reason* that brought him here, to Holland, to that boarding house; all his life since her death had been converging, though he did not know then, to that momentous instant.

"I think I know what I am going to do as soon as he gets trapped." he murmured.

She looked questioningly at him.

"I'm going to ask him *something*." he concluded.

She nodded, because she understood perfectly. He stared at his porcelain cup, now empty because he had finished the whole thing already, and in doing so he felt depressed. A cup which had been emptied made him feel that way; now he could see its clear bottom; the porcelain which had been so hot not five minutes ago, now was as cold as his wife's forehead. He wondered how many guests had drunk coffee from that same cup he was holding, and thought it obscenely impersonal and cold. Disgusted, he put that cup upon the table, and then shoved it slightly, until he was sure it was far from reach.

"It's about time." he said whilst standing up: "Let's hunt that ghost down."


10


He heard the key clicking in the door's latch and moved himself quickly under the bed. He did not want to be right there when *that* came in. He laid down upon the tiled cold floor, his eyes looking at that blackness of the bed frame, which had become, quite suddenly, his private ceiling; he closed his eyes tight and hoped for the worst to pass; he could hear now the door being shut and someone moving slowly in the flat. He tried to hold his breath.

"*Hello?*"

That unexpected voice startled him. That thing was not supposed to speak, not to mention to do so using a *well-known* voice. He realised that that thing, standing somewhere in the flat - the kitchen probably -, was, in fact, their neighbour; so nothing to be scared of, after all. But still, the mere idea of pushing himself out of that shelter, and meet her seemed preposterous. So he stayed down there, still holding his breath, not even daring to do the slightest move, wishing her to go away. Another *hello* would come, of course, because that neighbour was sure he was there; whether that was because she managed to perceive him or she had been told he would be *there*, he couldn't tell. He thought she was moving towards his bedroom, so he squeezed beneath the bed and put his right hand over his mouth to silence any sound. His eyes got used to that unnatural darkness, so he could see one slipper with its flat-sole facing up, resting clumsily over a couple of white long-forgotten socks; the other slipper was nowhere to be seen. "*Hello?*", it came again. He guessed she was by his bedroom's doorway, probably bending herself over to catch a better glimpse of the room's interior. A terrible thought shook him all over: maybe the blanket would allow her to see him sheltering under the bed. That was so because in order to get down there he had lifted it slightly and now he was unable to say for sure if he had put it back down. Thus, he opened his eyes, turning his head left vaguely, in order to find out. No; he had not. He could see a perfect gap which that blanket was supposed to cover; so that certainty, that dreadful realization, would finally come: he had been exposed to *her* all the time. However, she would say *Hello* just one more time, and then she would be headed for the flat's front door, without even trying to peer under the bed. Not much after that, the door would be slammed shut and he would be left alone.

It would be later on, one October rainy evening, when his mother would ask him about that; he could recall that perfectly well: his father was seated on that impressive black-furred armchair, smoking his cigar; she was peeling some potatoes for dinner; the telly was on because he was watching a Japanese cartoon called *Captain Herlock;* and he was seated on the sofa, holding the remote proudly. *Now tell me, darling,* she would start asking, *what possible reason would you have to do something like that?* At first he wasn't sure what she meant by that question. He was so concentrated on the way that certain *Captain Herlock* was vaporizing some improbable extraterrestrial creature with his laser-pistol, that it would be a question yet to be answered, even when he pushed the power button on the remote in order to turn off the TV. Thus, his mother would ask him again. At some point or another, he would understand; and yet it would be absolutely impossible to answer that question. His father would keep smoking his cigar impassibly, his deep dark eyes narrowed because of all the smoke; he would decide to remain silent because nothing was what he could tell his mother; and she would let the matter go, eventually.

*I miss you both*, he thought. That most certainly was: his father smoking those awful cigars, the house always stinking of tobacco, and that dreadful idea that someday, somehow, that old black-furred armchair would be set on fire: his father sometimes fell asleep seated on it holding the cigar lit up among his fingers; his mum would be the one in charge of keeping an eye on him for years on end, until his death. When he passed away, no-one would dare to seat on that armchair; from time to time, they both would look at it sadly, and more than once he would catch a glimpse of his mother crying silently. That empty armchair would symbolize how exposed anyone's life could be from then on. He wondered where it would be now; he thought his mother decided to get rid of it not long after his father's death. He could recall a framed gap on the floor where that old black-furred armchair had once stood; his mother would mop it restlessly until it shone.

It turned out the door was locked; so he had entered the room and had slid himself under the bed without hesitation. His landlady would be outside, mainly in the kitchen, waiting for him to get out. It was uncomfortable down there; he was grown up now, so there was not much room beneath the bed frame. He had to keep his head turned to one side, otherwise he would have touched the back of the bed frame with the tip of his nose. Instead of resting upon the tiled floor as when he was merely a kid hiding himself from his neighbour, now he laid upon a carpeted one, thus after two or three hours of unease waiting, he felt his back completely sweaty. He thought about his parents, the way his mother used to rescue him from his terrible nightmares; how his father kept smoking even when the doctor said to him he had cancer; and that incessant feeling of betraying them, all the time they asked him about his life, if he was with someone else, because in their own private and somehow simplistic world a man without love could not be happy at all. He pushed the bed frame slightly using his two hands, in a foolish attempt to make himself more room down there. This time, the blanket was covering him completely, and thus it was pitch back in there. From time to time he would use his own wristwatch, which was retro-illuminated, to light that small and suffocating space, evoking that single slipper resting all by itself, as if willing to go back to his long-ago childhood. Everybody was long-dead now, so he was more or less the last one standing. He was still young, but he felt old. He realised he had spent a lot of time since his wife passed away thinking about death. Curiously, instead of feeling depressed because of that, he smiled for the first time since then, liberated. Laying there, under that anonymous bed, he felt a bit sick because of the central heating, still on, warming that bedroom up. He wanted to ask her landlady to turn it off, but there was no way he could do that without revealing himself where he was sheltering; he did not want to take any chances, so he stayed down there resignedly. He had a quick look at his wristwatch once again. Sooner or later, that ghost would be back. He was completely sure he could hear the door getting open, and probably some weight upon the bed. Such an odd ghost in need of doing things the old way, he reckoned, was either a fool or a one without any ghostly-stuff previous experience. That was an old yet stupid theory he would discuss with his wife back then, during those old golden days of never-ending happiness. The first time it was her who would bring that matter up as if, in doing so, she would be piling additional arguments up to enforce her scepticism; they were seated on the sofa, listening to  the last Dark Sanctuary album, and he was almost sleepy: *Do you think someone who has just passed away, as a ghost, would be able to do things like, let's say, go trough a door without opening it before, right from the beginning?* He would consider for a while, but being sleepy it would be impossible to discuss about that properly; therefore they would put the matter at rest for a bit; in the days to come they would go back to those same weird theories. Maybe it was so; that writer had died quite suddenly, and now he was still wandering around the streets of that old medieval city, returning after a huge tourist stroll, exhausted, willing to have a shower and go to bed. And because he hadn't had neither the time nor the opportunity, he was unaware of the ghost ways of getting things done.

At some point, he fell asleep; maybe it was because of that awful central heating. He dreamed of his wife and his parents, and his old suicidal acquaintance would be there, as well. All of them were standing upright, looking and smiling stupidly at him. His mother wore a long black night gown so long he could not see her feet; his father was dressed in a magnificent smoking, a bit loose on his shoulders that he looked a bit uncomfortable; his acquaintance was completely naked, barely covering his thigh with that run out Liverpool calendar, which was still wrapped in that transparent foil, now completely stained with blood, and yet, despite his evident vulnerability, he seemed to be looking at him not the least bit embarrassed. He wanted to ask them why she was not among them, but he suddenly realized he did not know how to do that in dreams, therefore no words would be finally uttered.

Then, it came the squeaking: he awoke almost instantly, for a bit not remembering where he was, disoriented. The thick blackness surrounding him was certainly of no assistance at all; he could hear a door getting open but it took a whole minute to understand what *that* meant. His head was turned left, towards the door. He held his breath, waiting. The door was shut rapidly. For the best part of a minute, nothing was what he could hear; but then a slight clank came to his ears: something metallic, a key ring probably. He smiled; that has to be the keys, dangling, as he had foreseen, from the door's keyhole and clinking against one another. Then, some steps going towards the bed; he tried to shrink away from them, commanding his body to move itself to the right, but it

53

turned out it was impossible: there was no much room down there. He changed his mind and decided to stand still, listening. The steps seemed to stop somewhere near the bed, on his left. He perceived a puff and then nothing. That silence was so intolerable that he stupidly thought he had been detected, and he was waiting for the blanket to be brutally removed, and for some supernatural force to grab him and push him fiercely out of his so-obvious shelter. He closed his eyes in an unsuccessful attempt to skip a headache; an insurmountable throbbing pain was now at his left temple. He thought of an unexpected migraine, and why on earth he did not bring some painkillers with him before getting under the bed. The ghost could not be more than some centimetres away from him, and it was precisely because of his proximity that he could smell that fresh sweet scent. He opened his eyes, surprised, almost forgetting about his headache. *It can't be*, he said to himself. His head was still turned left, so he could see how the blanket seemed to be grazed. He envisaged some invisible presence passing by the bed, brushing the blanket to and fro, as if he was made of wind. A voice coming all of a sudden from the telly startled him. More about those Spanish cucumbers: it turned out Germany had been terribly mistaken, and those vegetables had nothing to do with the e.coli small crisis. At last, some good news. Then it came a slight thud; the remote falling upon the bed, he guessed. The steps seemed to get further from the bed, so he surmised the presence was going towards the bathroom. At some point or another, he could barely hear those steps, and he couldn't tell if that was because of the carpeted floor or because the ghost was starting to do things properly, maybe stepping on the floor one out of every two steps. Apart from the voices coming directly from the TV, now he did not hear anything else. Someone was talking about that cucumber European crisis quite excited, and then another voice would come out in no time in order to put that one at ease; amidst some irrational speeches about the different and unquestionable ways Spain was supposed to deal with Germany to sort that out, he heard the water running in the shower. Now that he thought that presence locked in the bathroom, he would allow himself some time to spare. His first thoughts would be related to that fragrance he had smelt as soon as the door got open. It was still there, everywhere. He recalled the first time he had smelt it: that first night, downstairs, in his very room, coming from that fresh yellow dahlias. Then, it was her perfume, no doubt about that. It seemed absolutely impossible that ghost could use the same elegant sweet perfume as his deceased wife. Mixed with that scent, there was a slight yet perceptible one only he could recall from her young white smooth skin. The steps came back, this time getting closer and probably returning from the bathroom. The ghost had had a shower, and now he was undoubtedly due to bed. He thought he would see the blanket being slightly lift from his left, because he was laying right under the place where the pillows were supposed to be, up there, upon the bed. However, that wouldn't happen. Whatever sort of ghost that was, it decided to lay down over the

54

blanket and, most likely, the bed-spread as well. He could hear the bed frame cracking faintly under the ghost weight whilst he was accommodating himself upon it. His both hands were put against the back of the bed frame instinctively, as if trying to avoid himself from being smashed. But it turned out that ghost did not weigh much, so he removed his hands and let them rest upon the hot carpeted floor, sighting. He waited. That thing was indeed breathing; now it was time for some averts on the TV. The entire bedroom came to a silence out of the blue; he thought the ghost was exhausted after a whole wandering-around-tourist-day, and decided to turn the TV off; those sparks and popping noises lasted for less than a second, but even so he would hear them pretty well. He closed his eyes in order to get rid of some little pinpricks which had appeared suddenly in his vision; that somehow unexpected headache was becoming something much worse: a migraine, maybe. He tried to stay calm. That scent of hers was more intense now. The ghost's breath went slow; he was probably asleep. He kept his eyes closed tight a bit longer, whilst thinking about what he would do next. The first idea had been to get out of under the bed, go towards the room's door straight away, grab the key ring, open the door carefully trying not to make the slightest noise, and lock it from the other side. Thus, the presence would end up trapped in there. *Not any-more,* he thought. He wanted that scent to be explained. He was in need of understanding why he could almost feel her presence in that room, not only because of that sweet smell, but in almost every single movement that ghost had performed. For instance, the way his wife used to rest over all the bedlinen during those previous misty minutes before the sleep because, she told him once, she hated the way the fabric brushed her skin uncontrollably; or his custom of letting the remote fall down upon the bed recklessly. But more importantly, he recalled, she was probably the only person he had ever met having showers every night, before going to bed, instead of having them after getting up early in the mornings. *It can't be,* he repeated to himself one more time. And yet, there the facts were. He opened his eyes again. The darkness where he was enclosed in helped him to avoid the migraine; the pinpricks had vanished. He was himself once again. Apart from the ghost's breath, there were no sounds in the bedroom. He listened: nothing. Carefully, he passed his left hand under the blanket and grabbed an edge of the wooden bed frame, all his fingers slid under the mattress but his thumb, which would stay under the bed frame, firmly, and pushed himself out. At first he was a bit dizzy; he had spent almost the whole day under the bed and with no much light. So it was normal to need some time for auto-adjustments. His eyes craved for more darkness, but he commanded them to open wide and resist; his second order would be for his groggy legs to awake; and so they would support his entire body once again, until he was standing upright and staring, astonished, at that white blanket resting irregularly upon some, yet unseen, human form. Where the human-breast was supposed to be, the blanket rose briefly, just to fall down smoothly, rhythmically, once again, clearly following the ghost's breath; the fabric would delimit a beautiful woman shape resting upon that bed, deeply asleep. She had found her way under that white clean blanket, after all. He stood in front of the bed; the first tear would show up, barely watering his left eye, but not rolling all his face down, not quite yet; he stood still, looking at that charming yet undefinable human-shape, breathless. He knew he was not allowed to touch the blanket, otherwise that form would be vaporised; that was the trick: the *connection* he was in pursuit of: that bedroom, that bed, the blanket, earthly goods now having a new and supernatural meaning: to keep the dead alive. That ghost was clearly that one of a woman, and therefore he was now sure it was *her*. So he was not scared, his headache was long-gone. He thought of so many plausible explanations why his wife was *there*; he tried to understand how, instead of that writer, the presence dwelling upstairs had turned out to be that one of *hers*; he considered different ways she could get the keys to get in; and yet, there she was; now that she was invisible, he thought her a new kind of beauty. Explanations apart, in fact, there was only one thing he could do right now. He had known all along, right since her death.

"I was right", he would say to that unseen human form resting upon that bed, now crying profusely, because of that *certainty*, that obvious resolution, that he was due to cease his own existence. Then, that form would move itself slightly to the right side of the bed, leaving the left one free: *his side*, he would realise. Not even death would make her forget about his habits. There would not be scrambling voices coming from the hereafter; not even funny lights or sparks hovering oddly in that room. He would lay down by her side, closing his eyes. She would caress his right cheek and she would follow his lips with an invisible index finger until the blackness eventually came.

*2011 Utrecht (The Netherlands),*
*Stamford (UK),*
*West Kirby (UK),*
*Ribes de Fresser (Girona),*
Cornellà de Llobregat (Barcelona)

Zeitfracht Medien GmbH
Ferdinand-Jühlke-Straße 7
99095 Erfurt, Deutschland
produktsicherheit@kolibri360.de

Druck:
CPI Druckdienstleistungen GmbH
im Auftrag der
Zeitfracht Medien GmbH
Ein Unternehmen der Zeitfracht - Gruppe
Ferdinand-Jühlke-Str. 7
99095 Erfurt